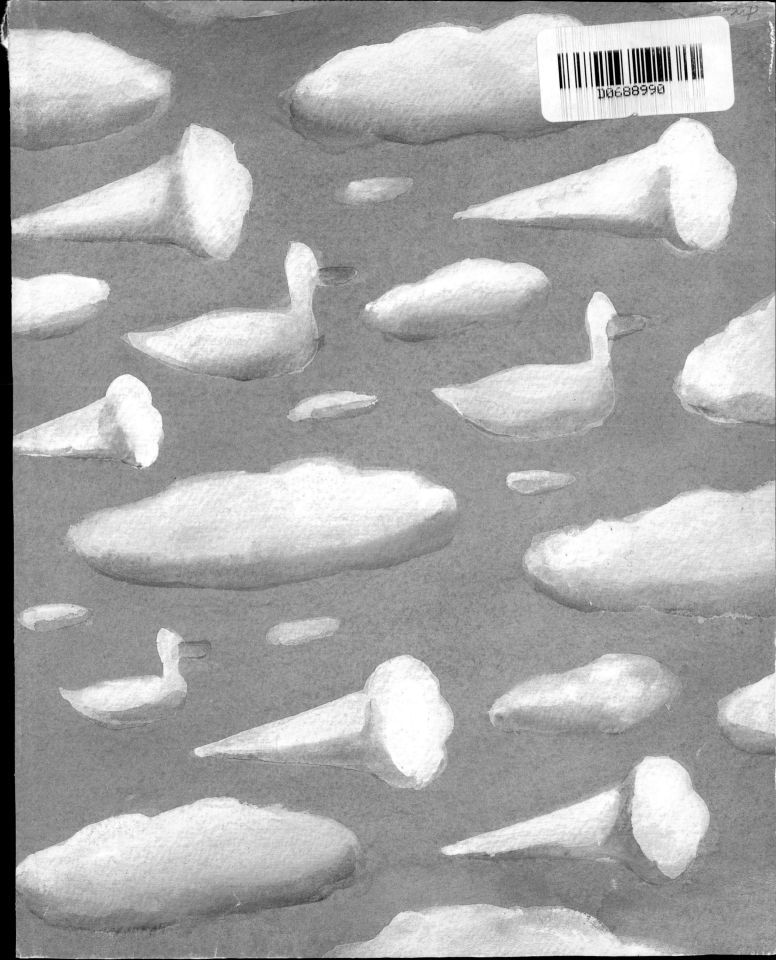

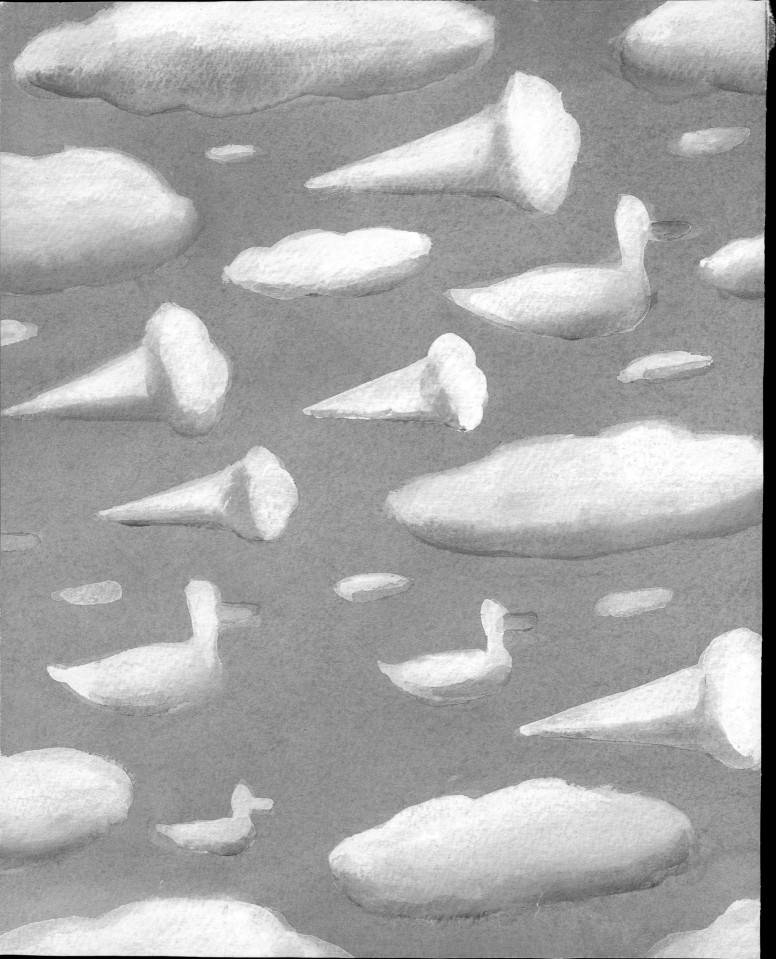

Dragon Is Coming!

Dragon
Com

s
ing!

Valeri Gorbachev

Harcourt Children's Books
Houghton Mifflin Harcourt New York 2009

Requests for permission to make copies of any part of the work should be submitted online
at www.harcourt.com/contact or mailed to the following address: Permissions Department,
Houghton Mifflin Harcourt Publishing Company, 6277 Sea Harbor Drive, Orlando, Florida
32887-6777.

Harcourt Children's Books is an imprint of Houghton Mifflin Harcourt Publishing Company.

www.hmhbooks.com

Library of Congress Cataloging-in-Publication Data
Gorbachev, Valeri.
Dragon is coming!/Valeri Gorbachev.
p.   cm.
Summary: Mouse frightens all of the animals she sees by shouting that a dragon is going to
eat the sun, and then come after them.
[1. Fear—Fiction.   2. Thunderstorms—Fiction.   3. Clouds—Fiction.   4. Mice—Fiction.
5. Domestic animals—Fiction.]   I. Title.
PZ7.G6475Dra   2009
[E]—dc22   2006101580
ISBN 978-0-15-205196-9

First edition
H G F E D C B A

Printed in Singapore

The illustrations in this book were done in pen-and-ink and watercolors
on watercolor paper.
The display and text type was set in Whitney.
Color separations by Colourscan Co. Pte. Ltd., Singapore
Printed and bound by Tien Wah Press, Singapore
Production supervision by Christine Witnik
Designed by Noon/designatnoon.com and Michele Wetherbee

To my granddaughters, Esther and Sarah Aliza

One summer day, Dog was watching the clouds. Some looked like fluffy white ducks in a blue lake. Some looked like ice-cream cones.

Suddenly, a dark cloud rolled in.

Wow. That big gray cloud looks like a dragon that will swallow the sun!

Dog's voice woke up Mouse, who was taking a nap nearby.

Aaaaaah!
Dragon is coming!

Mouse ran past the Goose Brothers.

The Goose Brothers flapped their wings and followed Mouse.
Soon they passed the Sheep Twins.

The Sheep Twins stamped their hooves, following Mouse and the Goose Brothers. Soon they met Mrs. Cow and Mrs. Pig.

Mrs. Cow and Mrs. Pig joined the stampede, following Mouse, the Goose Brothers, and the Sheep Twins right into the barn.

Mooooove!

Mouse closed the door. She locked the windows.
Then all the animals sat quietly in the darkness.

The animals huddled together and approached the door.

Squeeeeak!

CREATING
Keepsakes
SCRAPBOOK MAGAZINE

THE 1999
SCRAPBOOK
IDEA
BOOK

Oxmoor
House.

Creating Keepsakes™ The 1999 Scrapbook Idea Book

Copyright © 1998 Porch Swing Publishing, Inc.
Published by Oxmoor House, Inc.
Book Division of Southern Progress Corporation,
P.O. Box 2463, Birmingham, Alabama 35201

Library of Congress Catalogue Card number: 98-68073
ISBN: 0-8487-1900-X
Manufactured in the United States of America
First Printing 1998

Creating Keepsakes™ is a registered trademark of
Porch Swing Publishing, Inc., P.O. Box 2119, Orem, Utah 84059-2119, 888/247-5282.

WE'RE HERE FOR YOU!
We at Oxmoor House are dedicated to serving you with reliable information that expands your imagination and enriches your life. We welcome your comments and suggestions. Please write us at:

Oxmoor House, Inc.
Editor, Creating Keepsakes™
The 1999 Scrapbook Idea Book
2100 Lakeshore Drive
Birmingham, AL 35209
To order additional publications, call 205/877-6560.

OXMOOR HOUSE, INC.
Editor-in-Chief: Nancy Fitzpatrick Wyatt
Senior Crafts Editor: Susan Ramey Cleveland
Senior Editor, Editorial Services: Olivia Kindig Wells
Art Director: James Boone

PORCH SWING PUBLISHING, INC.
Publisher: Mark Seastrand
Editorial Director: Lisa Bearnson
Editor: Tracy White
Copy Editors: Jana Lillie, Kim Sandoval
Contributing Editors: Wendy Tams Hickman, Deanna Lambson
Design Director: Don Lambson
Designer: Joleen Hughes
Production Manager: Joani Hatch
Book Program Consultant: Maureen Graney
Index: Emily Haskell

Cover photo © Jade Albert

Front Cover: Scrapbook page designed by Becky Higgins of *Creating Keepsakes* magazine. **Supplies** *Background paper:* Solum World Paper; *Handmade paper:* Craf-T Pedlars; *Raffia:* Raffia Accents, Plaid; *Pens:* Zig Writer, EK Success; *Chalks:* Craf-T Products; *Flowers:* Nature's Pressed; *Other:* Becky stitched rope around the edges of cardstock.

Back Cover: **Top:** Scrapbook page designed by Carole Kamradt of The Paper Attic in Sandy, Utah. **Supplies** *Paper:* Over The Moon Press and Keeping Memories Alive; *Scissors:* Mini-Scallop edge, Fiskars; *Letter die cuts:* The Paper Attic; *Rubber stamps:* D.O.T.S.; *Computer font:* Scrap Casual, Lettering Delights, Inspire Graphics.
Bottom: Page designed by Jenny Jackson of Arlington, Virginia. **Supplies** *Rubber stamp:* D.O.T.S.; *Slot corner punch:* Family Treasures; *Red patterned paper:* Wrapping paper.

CONTENTS

90

A Smorgasbord of Ideas

Welcome to *The 1999 Scrapbook Idea Book,* *Creating Keepsakes'* annual showcase of the best brand-new, never-before-published scrapbook page ideas. So many scrapbookers loved last year's idea annual that this year, with the help of publisher Oxmoor House, we are offering it in hardcover format for the first time. We know you'll turn to this book again and again—there are 365 ideas, one for each day of the year!—and this sturdy binding will help keep the book and pages in tip-top shape through a year of good use.

The page layouts are larger this year, too, because readers wanted to get a closer look at how supplies were put together. We listened to your comments—let us know how you like what we've done this year.

The ideas in this book are the best of the best. They were carefully selected by our editors from thousands of great pages sent in by *Creating Keepsakes'* readers. Then, we organized them into chapters that describe the events that almost everyone takes pictures of: babies, kids, teens through adults, sports and recreation, vacations, moments with your family, holidays and Christmas.

This incredible idea book will make scrapbooking more fun—and it can save you money and time! How? If you've already found a page

with a color scheme and one or two special techniques you'd like to use for your latest batch of photos, simply jot down the items you need before your next trip to a craft supply store. This way, you'll buy exactly what you need. And how will it save you time? Well, here's how it has already saved me time.

As the editor of *Creating Keepsakes* magazine, I have the unique opportunity to attend scrapbook bashes all over the country. Our magazine's subscribers send me invitations, then every other month I randomly select one and show up at their bash—with scrapbook freebies in tote, of course! I spend a memorable evening scrapbooking, chatting, eating munchies and looking through other scrapbooks so I can get ideas for my own pages.

I love attending the parties, but getting my own scrapbook supplies ready to take to these bashes is another story. I always try to take my whole scrapbooking room, plus the kitchen sink.

What happens if I get the urge to create a Memorial Day page but don't have my medium circle punch to make the flowers? That would be a disaster!

I recently attended a bash at Karen Avila's house in Livermore, California. The week had been hectic, and the eve before my trip I was at the office frantically trying to get freebies together for Karen. I hadn't even begun to think about the pages I would create at the bash. Creative Editor Kim McCrary could see the frenzied look on my face and asked if she could help. Without a moment's hesitation I plopped some pictures from our vacation at Lake Powell on her lap and said, "Find a cute idea for me to copy, and grab the supplies I need to make the layout."

Because I was driving to California and my family would be with me, we couldn't fit my normal scrapbook stash in the car. This made pre-planned scrapbook pages—and a limit on supplies—a must. Fifteen minutes later Kim was back with a color copy of a Lake Powell idea and all the supplies. I was amazed! "How did you get this together so fast?" I asked. Kim explained how she'd been organizing the ideas for *The 1999 Scrapbook Idea Book* and remembered a cute Lake Powell page sent in by Karen Petersen. Because she had the layout in front of her, the supplies were easy to gather.

At most scrapbook bashes, it takes me almost an hour before I'm ready to start on each layout. This is because I have to carefully think of every detail on the page before I begin. At Karen's bash, the minute I sat down I was scrapbooking. I completed a four-page spread in record time. I used Karen's idea (see page 142) and adapted it to my own pictures (see my layout on this page). Thanks for the great idea, Karen!

With three kids, a husband, and a full-time job, I'm a busy person. People always ask me how I find time to scrapbook. Now you know my secret—seeing great ideas! I can pick out my supplies fast and get my pictures into our family's scrapbook while everyone's memories are still fresh. And somehow, I'm more likely to come up with my own original idea after looking at great pages than I am after staring at a blank sheet of paper! The hundreds of layouts in this book will help get your creative juices flowing, and your photos will fly into your scrapbook faster, and looking better, than ever before.

Speaking of "looking better," we also included a must-read chapter, "Create a Work of Art," on page 6 of the book. It shares some of the thinking behind the best scrapbook page designs. You can use these ideas when making up your own designs or when adapting ones made by others. At the heart of the chapter are principles that will make your photos the stars of your layouts.

You'll also love Deanna Lambson's essay, "Let Your Scrapbook Speak for Itself" (page 10). Deanna gives expert advice on how to capture the stories behind your photos, including how to record life's ordinary occurrences. She offers the insightful suggestion that telling about the person, not the portrait, will help you bring together over time the most loving, funny and treasured details about the family and friends you care so much about.

Enjoy this wonderful book, and have fun borrowing and adapting the ideas in it. And remember, creativity doesn't mean that you have to come up with an original idea every time you make a page. Creativity is taking a great idea and making it into your own unique masterpiece! ♥

Lisa Bearnson

Figure I. Thanks to a great idea from Karen Petersen, Lisa put her own twist on her Lake Powell photos. **Supplies** *Sun die cut:* Source unknown; *Stickers:* Stickopotamus; *Pen:* Micron Pigma, Sakura; *Memorabilia pocket:* 3L; *Idea to note:* Lisa tore her paper to mimic the rough edges of the rock formations at Lake Powell. She also collected some red sand from the beach and preserved it in a memorabilia pocket.

by Wendy Tams Hickman

Create a Work of Art

Did you know that as a scrapbooker, you're also a graphic designer? A graphic designer coordinates pictures, text, titles and color to communicate a message. That's exactly what you're doing when you create scrapbook layouts! Even though you can't list "Graphic Designer" on your resume, you can study and apply these eight basic artistic principles that will help you achieve great results.

UNITY

If you're preparing an Italian dinner, you don't serve tacos as a side dish, right? You choose other Italian dishes because that's what will complement your dinner. When working on your scrapbook layouts, you also need to incorporate this principle of unity. Unity means that all the elements of a design belong together.

In scrapbooking, the fundamental feeling of unity in a layout is created by photographs that relate to each other in theme or mood. Special days, such as a birthday or holiday, are great choices for themes, but themes can also be built around a collection of photographs from "ordinary" days with the same theme, a special pet, best friends or even family reunions (Figure 1).

8 basic
- - - - - - - - - - -
design
- - - - - - - - - - -
principles
- - - - - - - - - - -
for fabulous
- - - - - - - - - - -
layouts

EMPHASIS

Since the purpose of your scrapbook is to display and preserve photographs, the photographs should be the dominant factor of your layout, not the supporting design. Photos with sharp images, vivid colors and well-lit subjects create the perfect focal point.

You can emphasize your photos by using a variety of techniques. Size, color, position and shape all play an important role in emphasizing your photos. A large photo will be more dominant than a small photo, and a photo in the center

Before

After

Figure 1. While both girls are pictured in the photos in the "before" example, there is not one central theme to tie the photos together. Also note that it's difficult for poor-quality photos to be the dominant focal point of the layout. In the "after" example, Becky Higgins selected clear, bright and focused photos that have a more specific theme. *Note:* Becky utilized the principle of repetition by making her own yellow flower embellishments that mimic the yellow flower on the dress in the photos.

SUPPLIES "Before" example *Paper:* Paperbilities, MPR; *Punches:* McGill; *Pen:* Zig Writer, EK Success; *Colored pencils:* Prisma Color, Berol. **"After" example** *Paper:* Paperbilities, MPR; *Stickers:* Design Lines, Mrs. Grossman's; *Oval punch:* Marvy Uchida; *Circle punch:* McGill; *Pen:* Zig Writer, EK Success; *Colored pencils:* Prisma Color, Berol; *Idea to note:* Becky created the flowers by overlapping the oval punches and topping them off with a black circle in the middle.

Scissors: Provincial edge by Fiskars.

Let it Snow. Let it Snow. Let it Snow!!!

March 1997

Figure 2. The matting, size and placement make the top photo more dominant. *Page designed by Kim McCrary of Pleasant Grove, Utah.* **SUPPLIES** *Paper:* Close to my Heart; *Snowflake punches:* Family Treasures, McGill; *Computer font:* DJ Squirelly, Fontastic! 2, D.J. Inkers.

of your layout will stand out more than one that's in the corner (Figure 2).

The shape of your photos also plays an important role in their dominance. If you are going to crop a photo, remember that the most eye-pleasing shapes are usually simple. Rectangles and ovals, as well as circles and squares, are generally more natural and comfortable to the eye. Carving your photographs into stars, hearts and other complex shapes usually doesn't enhance them (Figure 3).

If the best shape choice doesn't seem obvious, experiment by placing different templates over the photograph, and choose the one that most quickly pleases you. When a variety of shapes might work for a photograph, place all of the cropped pictures on your layout and then decide which shape most effectively uses the available space.

PROPORTION

Proportion plays a big role in whether something is aesthetically pleasing. Without proper proportion, a design can look distorted, as well as shift the focus to something other than the pictures. One of the best ways to ensure that your layout is proportional is by examining your focal point—your photos. For example, if you have a picture of a person standing

on a beach several feet away from the camera, placing a large starfish die cut on your layout probably won't be your best bet.

Because the starfish has a greater proportional value than the person in the photo, your eye will go straight to the starfish. When choosing accents for your page, remember to pay attention to their size. A larger sticker or die cut might work well with a close-up photo of your son's face, but if the subject in the photo is relatively small, a large die cut will only diminish the photo's emphasis.

VARIETY

We all know that variety is the spice of life. The same holds true with your

scrapbook layouts! Variety is what makes them interesting. But just as in music theory, variation should be based on a theme (Figure 4). Embellishments such as stickers, punches and die cuts can go a long way in supporting your theme, but it is important to add these items with caution. They need to add to your layout and contribute to the mood or theme rather than distract or confuse the eye.

REPETITION

An easy way to add variety to your layouts while still maintaining your theme is to repeat the shapes, themes and colors found within your photographs. In doing so, you create rhythm and flow. For instance, if you have pictures of your family planting a flower garden, flower die cuts, punches or stickers will enhance your layout perfectly.

To further incorporate repetition in your layout, you may want to choose colors found within your photographs. For example, if your layout

Before

OUR happy FAMILY

COUSINS allgaier

MOM and DAD!

After

allgaier COUSINS AUGUST 1998

EMSLEY hannah WITH MOM♦DAD!

Figure 3. Note how the angular lines of the top photo in the "before" example are more prominent than the subjects of the photo. In an effort to crop out unnecessary background in the bottom photo, the artist has compromised the harmony of the photo. By utilizing eye-pleasing shapes in the "after" example, Becky Higgins kept the emphasis on the photographs and maintained their integrity.
SUPPLIES "Before" example *Heart punch:* Family Treasures; *Pen:* Zig Writer, EK Success. **"After" example** *Leaf punch:* McGill; *Die cut:* Accu-Cut Systems; *Pen:* Zig Writer, EK Success.

Before

After

Figure 4. Although the photos in the "before" example are unified, the embellishments are not. In the "after" example, Becky Higgins utilized embellishments that support the theme. *Note:* Becky also selected background colors that complement colors in the photographs. **SUPPLIES "Before" example** *Paper:* Creative Card Company; *Stickers:* Provo Craft; *Bear punch:* McGill. **"After" example** *Paper:* Papers By Design; *Scissors:* Deckle edge, Family Treasures; *Die cuts:* Ellison; *Sign and dog house:* Becky's own design; *Other:* Becky used string on her sign.

highlights pictures of a day at the beach, try using blues to reflect the color of the sky and the water, and neutral colors that resemble the sand. A wrong color choice generally draws attention away from your photographs (Figure 5). Try experimenting with different color combinations to find the perfect colors that will emphasize your photographs and bring out different photographic elements. Once you get the hang of it, repetition of color is an easy way to ensure that the elements of your layout belong together.

ECONOMY

A pleasing layout depends on the successful—and careful—use of the available space. An elegantly appointed dining room has only the essential elements—a dining table and chairs, a china cabinet and tasteful accents. Adding more and more furniture and decorations crowds the space and detracts from its beauty.

This principle of economy is also important in your layouts. When it comes to choosing which items to include on your layout, consider each one carefully. If any item disrupts the harmony of the page, remove it. Be willing to remove less important photographs when there isn't room. When deciding on embellishments, think "less is more" (Figure 6). For instance, hold off on red-and-green Christmas tree stickers if your page already looks great with more subdued white snowflakes.

MOVEMENT

When you look at a beautiful painting of a nature scene, your eyes don't just focus on one corner of the canvas—they move throughout the painting to take in the whole design. This sense of movement is also an important part of a scrapbook layout; it's the feeling of direction and flow that guides your eyes throughout the design.

A well-designed piece of art, photograph and even a newspaper, will generally follow a natural flow that mimics the letter Z. In general, the viewer's eye

Before

After

Figure 5. Compare these two layouts. In the "before" example, note that the embellishments have nothing to do with the photographs or each other, and the red background overpowers the photos. In the "after" example, Kim McCrary has selected a green paper that complements her son's vest. Because of this use of repetition, your eye comfortably focuses on the subject as opposed to the background. Careful placement of the leaf punch—also reflective of the natural setting of the photos—draws the eye throughout the page. **SUPPLIES "Before" example** *Stickers:* Mrs. Grossman's; *Computer font:* DJ Kool Skool, Fontastic! 2, D.J. Inkers. **"After" example** *Maple leaf punch:* Family Treasures.

gle items. Keep each of these factors in mind as you consider the placement of your photos, journaling, titles and embellishments. When you've planned your layout, envision placing it on a scale. Does it weigh the same side to side, top to bottom, and corner to corner? Wait to affix items to your page until you feel the layout is balanced.

FINALLY!

Of course you want your scrapbook to be a work of art. Now you can create artistic layouts based on the principles of design. Soon you'll be creating better layouts than you ever imagined possible. Hey, maybe you *can* get hired to do this! ♥

For more information on creating well-designed pages, check out Oxmoor House's Joy of Scrapbooking *by Lisa Bearnson and Gayle Humpherys, and Apple of Your Eye's* Core Composition *by Stacy Julian and Terina Darcey.*

Figure 6. With so many embellishments in the "before" example, it's hard for your eye to choose a focal point. Also note that there are too many styles of embellishments—daisies, hearts, stars, etc. By choosing a neutral background and using just daisies as embellishments in the "after" example, Gaylene Steinbach created a page where the photos are the stars. **SUPPLIES "Before" example** *Paper:* D.O.T.S.; *Stickers:* Frances Meyer; *Flower punch:* Family Treasures; *Circle punch* (¼"): Gem, McGill. **"After" example** *Paper:* D.O.T.S.; *Stickers:* Frances Meyer; *Flower punch:* Family Treasures; *Circle punch* (¼"): Gem, McGill.

will begin at the top-left corner, move to the top right, diagonally shift to the bottom-left corner and finally move to the right corner (Figure 7). As a scrapbooker, you can also create this natural flow and movement. Keep in mind that you, as the artist, are allowed to lead the viewers' eyes. An easy way to facilitate this may be to emphasize your primary focal point, perhaps by double matting it. Then move the eye to your secondary focal point (this could be achieved with a single mat) and so on. Another technique for creating visual movement is by overlapping or connecting some photos.

BALANCE

There are two main kinds of balance: symmetry and asymmetry. In a symmetrically balanced layout, the elements are arranged equally left and right, and top and bottom. Asymmetry, on the other hand, creates a more informal balance where the elements are not the same on each side of the layout (Figure 7).

Attaining balance doesn't necessarily relate to the positioning of your photos. It's important to keep in mind that

certain elements such as color, texture and size can also affect balance. Bright colors and dark colors are heavier than neutral colors. Textured items carry weight, as do large items. In addition, items in a group weigh more than sin-

Figure 7. This two-page spread is a perfect example of a Z flow. Your eye starts at the top left-hand corner and is moved along by the flow of the title to the pictures in the top right-hand corner. The pipes that extend from the photo diagonally guide your eyes to the bottom left-hand photo. Because of this photo's angle, your eyes move to the journaling and the final photo in the bottom right-hand corner. *Note:* Although the elements on each side of the layout don't mirror each other, both sides weigh the same. *Page designed by Deanna Lambson of Sandy, Utah.* **SUPPLIES** *Pen:* Zig Opaque Writer and Zig Writer, EK Success; *Colored pencils:* Prisma Color, Berol.

by Deanna Lambson

Let Your Scrapbook
Speak for Itself

I've got the ultimate three-part challenge for you. Are you ready? Clutch your scrapbook with one arm, then hook a friend (or anyone who hasn't seen your album) with the other and sit on the sofa together. Here's the first part of the challenge. As you look at your scrapbook, you can't say a word. You're not allowed to point, laugh or talk about your photos. Go ahead—try it! Can't do it? You're not alone. For me it's utterly impossible! I can't stand for anyone to look at my photos without me, because I want to add the play-by-play commentary.

Here's part two of the challenge:

Turn through the pages of your life again, but this time say whatever comes to your mind. Go ahead and talk to your friend, smile, point, reminisce—tell all the little details. Explain why you took the photo, how fun the event was, and what has happened to that special person since the photo was taken. You may find yourself pointing to a photo and saying something like, "Right after we took this Thanksgiving picture of the family, the turkey caught on fire and we feasted on Chinese take-out."

4 ways
- - - - - - - - - -
to tell
- - - - - - - - - -
the tale

Why do you and I have to "talk" through our scrapbooks? Because there are countless stories and feelings that the photos don't tell (Figure 1). The memories involve so much more than the brief flashes captured on film. Remember all of those details that came out of your mouth while talking to your friend? The third part of the scrapbooker's challenge is to capture those exact words in midair and press them onto your scrapbook pages. It sounds magical, but it can be done—easily! If you've ever avoided journaling on your pages because you just couldn't think of what to write, keep reading. I'll share four simple ways to capture your stories and emotions on your scrapbook pages.

❶ Extend the borders of your photos. I don't mean to grab a photo and try to stretch it. Just take a particular photo and mentally extend each side to see the bigger picture (Figure 2). What would you see if you walked around the corner? What was

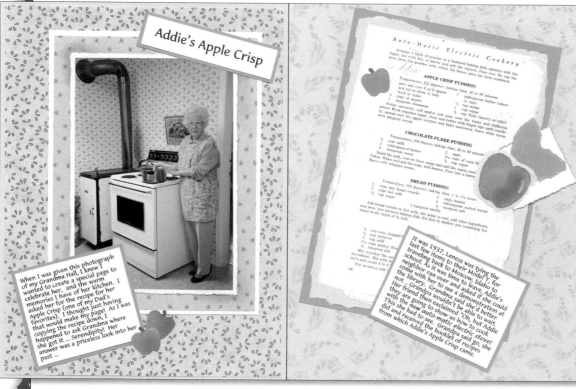

Addie's Apple Crisp

Figure 1. One photo may open the floodgates for many wonderful memories. If you take the time to ask questions, you may be surprised at the stories you'll hear. *Page designed by Stacy Julian, co-author of* Core Composition. **Supplies** *Paper:* Wubie Prints and Provo Craft; *Apple punch:* Marvy Uchida; *Apple rubber stamp:* D.O.T.S.; *Chalk:* D.O.T.S.; *Idea to note:* Stacy color-copied Addie's recipe and included it on her scrapbook page.

Scissors: Victorian edge by Fiskars.

Figure 2. If you ask yourself what prompted you to take the photos, you'll know exactly the story to write on your page. *Page designed by Karen Newmiller of Sandy, Utah.* **Supplies** *Paper:* Wubie Prints; *Banner die cut:* Accu-Cut Systems; *Seeds:* From the bird feeder, of course.

happening in the world, and what were you feeling in your heart? Pretend that your photo is only one frame in a video. Continue to watch your "photo video" as the story unfolds. Rewind to see what happened just before the photo was taken, just after and later on that day.

Janice Dixon, in her book *The Art of Writing Scrapbook Stories,* reminds us that many remarkable things happen when a photographer isn't around. Be sure to tell the whole story, not just the instant that was captured in the photo (Figure 3). If you're scrapbooking photos from past years, be sure to share your current perspective, as well as the details of the photos. It's fascinating to realize how times change, to see comparisons and understand how we've grown.

2 Record the ordinary. Almost every scrapbooker likes to include exciting memories and unusual stories in his or her album. But don't overlook the power of a few ordinary details to carry you back in time. Can you picture in your mind's eye the bedspread of your childhood? These ordinary, insignificant details of your life will be the nostalgic memories of tomorrow (Figure 4).

Bob Greene, in his book *To Our Children's Children,* invites us to "wander the golden corridors of memory. No detail is unimportant," he reminds. "The smallest things make up the richness of the big picture. Writing what your parents' wallpaper looked like may set off a flood of other memories."

Louise Plummer, author of *Thoughts of a Grasshopper,* worries that as humans we don't appreciate the fabric of our own lives with its details and repetition. She suggests a technique called the "five-minutes-a-day journal." This idea works great for scrapbookers who are searching for those simple details to include in an album. Set a kitchen timer for five minutes and begin writing. Just let your mind wander. You'll find yourself mentioning details

Figure 3. "Going beyond the photos" means telling what happened before, after, or as in this example, what happened in between the photos (poor Keaton!). *Page designed by Allison Myers of Memory Lane in Mesa, Arizona.* **Supplies** *Colored pencil:* Prisma Color, Berol; *Square punch:* Family Treasures; *Paper:* The Paper Patch; *Pen:* Zig Writer, EK Success. *Idea to note:* Allison used a circle cutter and a square punch to create her Viewmaster slide.

Figure 4. Don't forget to record the priceless bits and pieces of everyday life, even if it means taking pictures of your child's stuffed friends. *Page designed by Allison Myers of Memory Lane in Mesa, Arizona.* **Supplies** *Paper:* Kangaroo & Joey; *Colored pencil:* Prisma Color, Berol; *Letter template:* Pebble Tracers, Pebbles in my Pocket.

such as how much you love early mornings in the spring or what parts of the house need repair. Each detail illustrates an intimate look at your life. You can select bits and pieces of your five-minute journal to include in your

scrapbook and it only takes—you guessed it—five minutes!

Louise also suggests making lists to include on your album pages. List all the teachers you ever had or all the stores you like to shop. Consider something as simple as listing the television programs you've watched this week or what you find hidden in the couch cushions. Each of these bits of information is part of your everyday life and makes up who you are.

The next time you're scrapbooking photos of your children at play, try this terrific journaling idea. Dump out the contents of the entire toy box (if your children are like mine, they've already done it for you) and make a list of each toy's approximate price. I know my children will smile when they remember creatures from Beast Wars and Beanie Babies just as I do when I recall my hours with Lite Brite and Hippity-Hops.

❸ Tell about the person, not the portrait. How many times have you mounted a wonderful portrait on your scrapbook page and written only the name and date? Although it's always

important to record the "who" and "when," sometimes we fail to include the "why" and "how." Remember to include the details that make that person unique. What were his or her hobbies and profession? What impact did this person have on your life? When scrapbooking your child's next school portrait, write about favorite lunchroom menus or games to play at recess (Figure 5). Along with a family portrait you could include a special family tradition, the words to songs that you always sang in the car, or even the events surrounding the birth of each child.

Valerie Dellastatious, marketing director for *Creating Keepsakes* magazine, recalls that as a child she once asked her great-grandmother why she had "cracks" in her face. This wise woman proceeded to tell her what it was like to grow old. Valerie learned how wrinkles form and heard how it feels to struggle to walk. They even discussed the age spots on the back of her grandmother's hands as Valerie touched each one. Years later, when Valerie wanted to scrapbook a photo of her great-grandmother, she knew exactly what experience to include on the page. Wouldn't it be a shame not to include that story simply because it didn't occur when the photo was taken?

15 Journaling Jump-starters

If you'd like some sure-fire journaling ideas, snip this section and keep it in the front of the album you're working on. Whenever you're stumped for a caption or story, simply answer one of the following questions. At least one answer (probably more) will perfectly complement the page you're working on.

① What happened just before or after this photo was taken?
② How did you feel on that day? Do you feel differently today?
③ Why is this person(s) so special to you? Describe his or her personality and relationship to you.
④ Did this photo involve a tradition? Tell about this or other traditions.
⑤ What does this photo or experience tell about you or your family?
⑥ What was happening around you when this photo was taken? Record current events, a description of the seasons, or a description of the home.
⑦ Share a memory from your childhood that relates to this event—a favorite vacation, an experience at school, or your best friends from your youth.
⑧ What makes a terrific day for you? What things ruin your day?
⑨ How have the people or places changed over the years since the photo was taken? (Is your house still there or is it an office complex?)
⑩ Was this picture part of an everyday activity? Describe what ordinary events fill your day from your route to work to your house-cleaning routine.
⑪ Could another person share a story or perspective about this occasion? Capture his or her exact words or actual handwriting if possible.
⑫ What was the most memorable or humorous experience you ever had with this person?
⑬ Ask "why" questions, such as, "Why did you take the photo?" "Why do you like the photo?" or "Why are they doing what they're doing in the photo?"
⑭ What are the words to a song, poem or thought that remind you of that particular time in life?
⑮ Describe the setting of the photo using all of your senses.

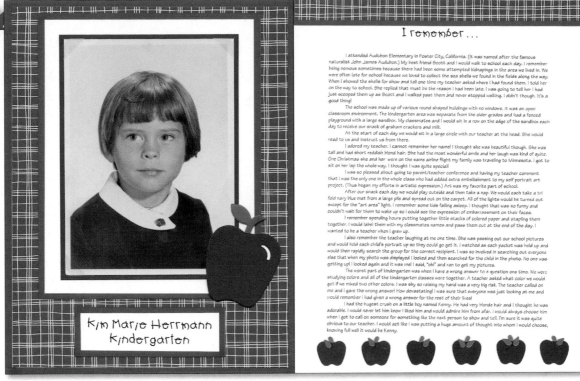

I remember...

I attended Audubon Elementary in Foster City, California. (It was named after the famous naturalist John James Audubon.) My best friend Scott and I would walk to school each day. I remember being nervous sometimes because there had been some attempted kidnapings in the area we lived in. We were often late for school because we loved to collect the sea shells we found in the fields along the way. When I showed the shells for show and tell one time my teacher asked where I had found them. I told her on the way to school. She replied that must be the reason I had been late. I was going to tell her I had just scooped them up as Scott and I walked past them and never stopped walking. I didn't though. It's a good thing!

The school was made up of various round shaped buildings with no windows. It was an open classroom environment. The kindergarten area was separate from the older grades and had a fenced playground with a large sandbox. My classmates and I would sit in a row on the edge of the sandbox each day to receive our snack of graham crackers and milk.

At the start of each day we would sit in a large circle with our teacher at the head. She would read to us and instruct us from there.

I adored my teacher. I cannot remember her name! I thought she was beautiful though. She was tall and had short reddish blond hair. She had the most wonderful smile and her laugh was kind of quite. One Christmas she and her were on the same airline flight my family was traveling to Minnesota. I got to sit on her lap the whole way. I thought I was quite special!

I was so pleased about going to parent/teacher conference and having my teacher comment that I was the only one in the whole class who had added extra embellishment to my self portrait art project. (Thus began my efforts in artistic expression.) Art was my favorite part of school.

After our snack each day we would play outside and then take a nap. We would each take a tri fold navy blue mat from a large pile and spread out on the carpet. All of the lights would be turned out except for the "art area" light. I remember some kids falling asleep. I thought that was so funny and couldn't wait for them to wake up so I could see the expression of embarrassment on their faces.

I remember spending hours putting together little stacks of colored paper and stapling them together. I would label them with my classmates names and pass them out at the end of the day. I wanted to be a teacher when I grew up.

I also remember the teacher laughing at me one time. She was passing out our school pictures and would hold each child's portrait up so they could go get it. I watched as each packet was held up and would then rapidly search the group for the correct recipient. I was so involved in searching out everyone else that when my photo was displayed I looked and then searched for the child in the photo. No one was getting up! I looked again and it was me! I said, "oh!" and ran to get my pictures.

The worst part of kindergarten was when I have a wrong answer to a question one time. We were studying colors and all of the kindergarten classes were together. A teacher asked what color we would get if we mixed two other colors. I was so shy so raising my hand was a very big risk. The teacher called on me and I gave the wrong answer! How devastating! I was sure that everyone was just looking at me and would remember I had given a wrong answer for the rest of their lives!

I had the hugest crush on a little boy named Kenny. He had very blonde hair and I thought he was adorable. I would never let him know I liked him and would admire him from afar. I would always choose him when I got to call on someone for something like the next person to show and tell. I'm sure it was quite obvious to our teacher. I would act like I was putting a huge amount of thought into whom I would choose, knowing full well it would be Kenny.

Kim Marie Herrmann
Kindergarten

Figure 5. Many wonderful memories occur when no photographer is there to snap a picture. Let your mind wander and reminisce. Even the smallest details make up the richness of the picture. *Page designed by Kim McCrary of Pleasant Grove, Utah.* **Supplies** *Paper:* Northern Spy; *Die cut:* Ellison; *Teardrop punch:* McGill; *Apple punch:* McGill; *Computer font:* DJ Crayon, Fontastic!, DJ. Inkers. *Idea to note:* Kim used the teardrop punch to create the leaves on the apple.

The most important words to record on your pages may be those that describe a personality. Recently, my husband's grandmother died. As we visited one evening about grandma, a tear slid down my husband's cheek. "Our children will never know her," he said. My first response was, "Then we have to tell them." Our scrapbook is the perfect place to tell about grandma—how she always kept lemon sandwich cookies in the bottom drawer of her white metal cabinets, how she loved bright pink and yellow, and how she collected ceramics and wore a flower corsage every Sunday. Although our photos of grandma are of her later years, our children will come to know her as we include in our scrapbook stories and experiences from her youth that were never photographed.

❹ **Get others to write for you.** This may sound like a cop-out but it's actually a wonderful way to get more facts. When a family member or friend shares his or her perspective, you'll be able to enjoy memories that you didn't experience personally. You'll also have a won-

derful keepsake of that person's handwriting and unique personality.

One day, while working on my scrapbook, my in-laws dropped by. I handed my father-in-law a piece of stationery and asked him to describe his father, Apolles, who died long before my husband was born. A few minutes later he handed me a full page about Apolles—how he loved children and could break in any wild horse. It was filled with stories that I would have never known.

Stacy Julian, co-author of *Core Composition,* reminds us that the possibilities are endless—and so meaningful—when we include others' words. Ask your children to describe a family trip or explain what mom and dad do at work. (Wouldn't it be entertaining to hear what your children think you do at work?) Consider having an older neighbor write everything he or she recalls about the home you live in. Try asking your roommate to write the 10 things about you that make you impossible to live with. How about asking your parents to write how they see themselves in you? These perspectives are priceless in telling the story of your life.

Now that you've taken on the scrapbooker's challenge with these four ideas, you'll know how to tell the stories that go beyond the photos. Far into the future, your family and friends will pick up your albums and hear your voice as if you were sitting right beside them on the sofa. After all, you wouldn't want them looking at your albums without you! ♥

For more information on telling your life stories, look for these great books:

♥ *To Our Children's Children* by Bob Greene, Doubleday, New York, 1993

♥ *The Book of Myself* by Carl and David Marshall, Hyperion, New York, 1994

♥ *1,400 Things to Be Happy About* by Barbara Ann Kipfer, Workman Publishing, New York, 1990

♥ *The Art of Writing Scrapbook Stories* by Janice T. Dixon, Mt. Olympus Publishing, Salt Lake City, 1998

♥ *Thoughts of a Grasshopper* by Louise Plummer, Deseret Book, Salt Lake City, 1992

♥ *How to Write Your Autobiography* by Patricia Ann Case, Woodbridge Press Publishing, Santa Barbara, 1995

24th July Parade. Jacob Raggedy Andy. Nick a pirate, Tyler is an aladin. morgan in red skirt.

PARADE

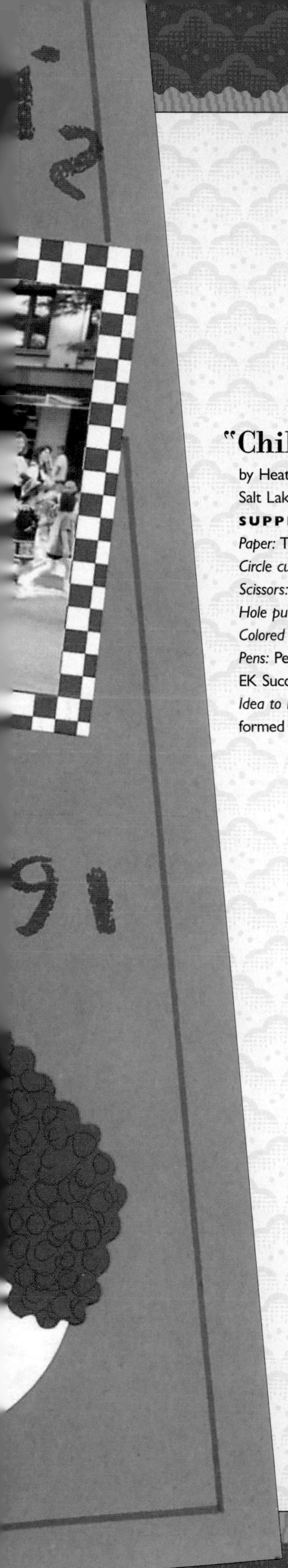

CANDID KIDS

"Children's Parade"

by Heather Spurlock
Salt Lake City, Utah

SUPPLIES
Paper: The Paper Patch
Circle cutter: Fiskars
Scissors: Scallop edge, Fiskars
Hole punch (¼"): Gem, McGill
Colored pencils: Prisma Color, Berol
Pens: Pentel; Zig Memory System,
EK Success
Idea to note: The folded hat was
formed from a square of newspaper.

Oh, to be a kid again—swinging on a

tire swing during a hot summer

afternoon, playing hide-and-go-seek

late into the evening, getting butterflies

in your stomach on the first day

of school, and anticipating your

first piano recital. Gather some

exciting ways to capture these unique

moments of youth in this section.

Scissors: Ripple edge by Fiskars.

"My Sequoia Tree"

by Debi Boler
Newport Beach, California

SUPPLIES
Paper: The Paper Patch
Scissors: Peaks edge, Fiskars
Corner edger: Art Deco, Fiskars
Font: DJ Desert, Fontastic!, D.J. Inkers
Tree punch: McGill
Template: Provo Craft
Pen: Zig Millennium, EK Success

August 1997
I got a sequoia tree as my souvenir from our trip and me and Mommy planted it. Each year, we're gonna take my picture by my tree and see how tall it gets – and see how tall I get!

Christopher Alan Wendel
Oct 1, 1997
Bar Ridge Canyon

"Christopher Alan Wendel"

by Katie Wendel
Down Memory Lane
Brigham City, Utah

SUPPLIES
Paper: The Paper Company
Die cuts: Ellison
Pen: Zig Writer, EK Success

"Swingin'"

by Paula Lietzke
Greenville, Wisconsin

SUPPLIES
Stickers: Mrs. Grossman's
Die cuts: Accu-Cut Systems; Ellison
Pen: Zig Writer, EK Success

swingin'

It's summer time in Utah! We love to play outside – when it's not too hot and this swing, hanging from the deck, is a favorite.

Steffi – nearly 3!

Nolan – 8½ months

"Wanted, Kid Austin"

by Tawna Hansen
Vauxhall, Alberta, Canada

SUPPLIES
Paper: Paper Pizazz, Hot Off The Press
Hat stationery: Source unknown
Scissors: Stamp edge, Fiskars

Stickers: Frances Meyer
Stencils: Provo Craft
Pens: Micron Pigma, Sakura
Font: PT Barnum BT, Corel WordPerfect 8
Idea to note: Tawna used a candle to burn the edges of the wanted sign and one of the photo mats.

"An Old Fashioned Summer Day"

by Carole Jackman
Nature's Pressed
Orem, Utah

SUPPLIES
Pressed flowers: Nature's Pressed

Brit, Reagan, & Kelton had their first watermelon of the year with Amanda & Cassadie Ropp.

BRITIAN

KELTON

KELTON JUST WASN'T SURE WHAT END SHE WAS SUPPOSE TO EAT

WATERMELLON MMM... GOOD

REAGAN

"I Love Watermelon"
by Cindy Barr
Meridian, Idaho

SUPPLIES

Paper: D.O.T.S.; Close to my Heart
Scissors: Deckle edge, Family Treasures;
Pinking and Mini-Pinking edges, Fiskars

Font: DJ Signpost and DJ Doodlers, Fontastic!,
D.J. Inkers
Templates: Source unknown
Pens: Tombow

I ♥ watermellon

JUNE 1997

BROGANS FIRST WATERMELLON

BROGAN

JUNE 1997

Grandpa's Watermelon

Yum!

Yum!

"Grandpa's Watermelon"

by Vicki Garner
Memories By Design
Layton, Utah
SUPPLIES
Paper: Windows of Time; The Paper Patch
Font: Times Bold, Print Artist

"Blowing Kisses"

by Marlene Bixenman
Ontario, California
SUPPLIES
Paper: Marlene's own design
Stickers: Mrs. Grossman's
Punches: Family Treasures
Circle cutter: Fiskars
Template: Creative Memories
Pens: Gelly Roll, Sakura
Idea to note: Marlene used a circle cutter to make the cover of the fan and then free-handed the base of the fan. The blades were made with a small heart template.

"Savannah"

by Angie McGoveran
Festus, Missouri

SUPPLIES
Paper: Keeping Memories Alive
Font: DJ Chunky, Inspirations, D.J. Inkers

"Lazy Daze of Summer"

by Tami Comstock
Pocatello, Idaho

SUPPLIES
Daisy stationery: Frances Meyer
Paper: The Paper Patch

Pens: Zig Writer, EK Success
Idea to note: Tami used the "Cookie Hollow" font from Print Artist to create the title. She electronically reversed the image and printed on the backside of the printed paper. Then she simply cut out each letter!

"Sam and Riley"

by Jane Nicolay
Fairway, Kansas
SUPPLIES
Paper: The Paper Patch
Stickers: Making Memories
Scissors: Jumbo Deckle edge,
Family Treasures
Circle punch: Fiskars
Hole punch: Punch Line, McGill
Idea to note: Jane created "overall buttons"
with her circle and hole punches.

"Toothless"

by Sharon Lewis
Memory Lane
Mesa, Arizona
SUPPLIES
Paper: The Paper Patch; Frances Meyer;
Memory Press
Scissors: Leaf edge, Fiskars
Corner punch: Victorian, All Night Media
Stickers: Mrs. Grossman's
Letter template: Frances Meyer

QUINN
1997

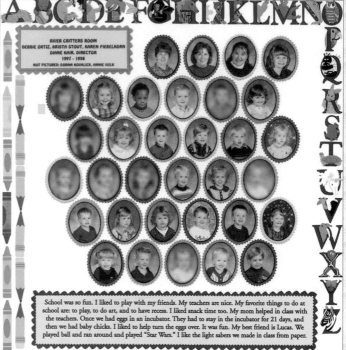

RIVER CRITTERS ROOM
DEBBIE ORTIZ, KRISTA STOUT, KAREN FIEBELKORN
DIANE KAIR, DIRECTOR
1997 - 1998
NOT PICTURED: DONNA KOVALICK, ANNIE VOLK

School was so fun. I liked to play with my friends. My teachers are nice. My favorite things to do at school are: to play, to do art, and to have recess. I liked snack time too. My mom helped in class with the teachers. Once we had eggs in an incubator. They had to stay in the incubator for 21 days, and then we had baby chicks. I liked to help turn the eggs over. It was fun. My best friend is Lucas. We played ball and ran around and played "Star Wars." I like the light sabers we made in class from paper.

"Quinn"

by Amy Carrell
Des Moines, Iowa

SUPPLIES

Scissors: Seagull, Mini-Pinking and Dragonback edges, Fiskars
Stickers: Mrs. Grossman's; Frances Meyer; Sandylion
Pens: LePlume, Marvy Uchida
Ruler: Borderlines, Creative Memories
Idea to note: Amy found a great way to showcase an entire class.

"The Apple of My Eye"

by Debi Boler
Newport Beach, California

SUPPLIES

Paper: Close to My Heart; The Paper Patch
Scissors: Deckle edge, Fiskars
Template: Pebbles in my Pocket
Pens: Zig Clean Color, EK Success
Stamps: Rubber Stampede

April 1997

Our neighbor parked a school bus in front of our house & she let the kids get on it. They thought it was COOL!

SCHOOL BUS
EMERGENCY DOOR

THE KIDS ON THE BUS GO UP AND DOWN

"The Kids on the Bus"

by Kerri Bradford
Orem, Utah

SUPPLIES

Paper: The Paper Patch
Scissors: Wave and Deckle edges, Fiskars
Ruler: Borderlines, Creative Memories
Die cuts: Creative Memories
Pens: Micron Pigma, Sakura
Letter stickers: Sticklers

"Kindergarten Keepers"

by Vicki Garner
Memories By Design
Layton, Utah

SUPPLIES

Paper: The Paper Patch; Suzy's Zoo
Font: First Grader, Print Artist
Idea to note: Vicki used elements of Suzy's Zoo stationery to create these pages.

KEEPERS

Knowlton
Elementary
1988-89
Kindergarten AM

KINDERGARTEN

FIRST DAY OF PRESCHOOL!

"First Day of School"

by Deb Day
Coon Rapids, Minnesota

SUPPLIES

Paper and cutouts: Hot Off The Press
Stickers: Creative Memories; Fiskars
Clip art: Cut and Copy, D.J. Inkers
Pens: LePlume, Marvy Uchida

"Crayola Crayon Factory"

by Angelyn Bryce
West Chester, Pennsylvania

SUPPLIES

Paper: Angelyn's own design
Stickers: Frances Meyer
Pens: Zig Millennium, EK Success
Idea to note: Have fun "scribbling" a design for a fun background paper.

CRAYOLA CRAYON FACTORY
We toured the factory in Bethlehem, PA with Kathryn Lateur and her children. Kathryn is Dana's friend visiting from Belgium. We had lots of fun!
November, 1997

WRITING BAT STORIES FOR HALLOWEEN.

ZACH SHARING CUPCAKES ON HIS BIRTHDAY. ALSO - THE QUILT THE KIDS MADE FOR CHARITY.

LOOKING AT PICTURES OF ZACH ON HIS VIP POSTER - BIRTHDAY.

GOING THROUGH THE "SPANKING" MACHINE FOR HIS BIRTHDAY.

MARCH 11, 1997. STUDENT OF THE DAY FOR DOING WONDERFULL WORK IN SCHOOL. THIS WAS HIS SECOND ONE FOR THE YEAR.

THE 3 LITTLE PIGS, THE BIG BAD WOLF (ZACH) AND LITTLE RED RIDING HOOD.

THE FIRST GRADE STUDENTS SPREAD CHRISTMAS CHEER IN REINDEER DISGUISE FOR THE WHOLE STUDENT BODY.

THE DENTAL PLAY

THROUGH THE YEAR.

SCHOOL

FIRST GRADE

"First Grade"

by Kerri Bradford
Orem, Utah

SUPPLIES

Paper: Creative Memories
Scissors: Clouds edge, Fiskars
Stickers: Frances Meyer; Provo Craft
Letter stickers: Creative Memories

Templates: Provo Craft
Die cuts: Creative Memories
Idea to note: Kerri used the outside edge of the ABC stickers and placed them on the cranberry checked paper. She then cut them out and adhered them to the page.

"Last Day of School"

by Kerri Bradford
Orem, Utah

SUPPLIES

Paper: Creative Memories
Stickers: Provo Craft; Frances Meyer
Scissors: Clouds and Colonial edges, Fiskars
Idea to note: Kerri included her son's completion certificate on her layout. Try placing the title down the side of the page as a border.

"THE CLASS"

Alpine School District

This Certifies That

Zachary Bradford

has been advanced from the _1st_ grade to the _2nd_ grade.

Given as _Bonneville Elementary_ School _July 2, 1997_

Good Job!

JORDAN FISHER, JENNI DRIVIT, GENTRY CROFT, TAP & TRAVIS FULLER, AND ZACHARY.

FOREVER FRIENDS.

ZACHARY RECIEVING AN AWARD FOR TRYING VERY HARD IN CLASS.

ZACH WITH IAN ANDERSON.

ZACH WITH TRAVIS FULLER.

ZACH & MRS. KITTO.

LAST DAY OF SCHOOL

Festival of Flowers

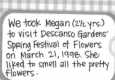

We took Megan (2½ yrs.) to visit Descanso Gardens' Spring Festival of Flowers on March 21, 1998. She liked to smell all the pretty flowers.

"Festival of Flowers"

by Lori Hodgson
Claremont, California

SUPPLIES

Paper: Frances Meyer

Scissors: Deckle edge, Fiskars

Craft punches: Marvy Uchida (snowflake, sun); Family Treasures (star, swirl); McGill (mini flower)

Hole punch: Gem, McGill

Pens: Zig Clean Color, EK Success; Micron Pigma, Sakura

Idea to note: To create a full-flowered effect, Lori overlapped sun, star and snowflake punches.

"First Communion"

by Kathy Maghini
Bristol, Connecticut

SUPPLIES

Paper: Paper Pizazz, Hot Off The Press

Scissors: Clouds and Mini-Pinking edges, Fiskars

Sticker: Provo Craft

Die cut: Source unknown

Cross punch: Marvy Uchida

Pen: Micron Pigma, Sakura

Idea to note: Kathy included a greeting card given to her daughter.

"Scouts"

by Jewelene Holverson
Pocatello, Idaho

SUPPLIES

Scissors: Peaks edge, Fiskars
Pens: LePlume, Marvy Uchida
Rubber stamp: D.O.T.S.
Scout kerchief: Jewelene's own design

"Daisy Girl Scouts"

by Marsha Peacock
Jacksonville, Florida

SUPPLIES

Daisy stationery: NRN Designs
Scissors: Jumbo Scallop and Deckle edges, Family Treasures; Clouds edge, Fiskars
Sticker: Frances Meyer
Photo corners: Source unknown
Pens: 3D Crystal Laquer, Sakura; Zig Opaque Writer, EK Success
Flower leaves and stems: Marsha's own design

"Oreo"

by Kim Cook
The Heartland Paper Co.
Bountiful, Utah

SUPPLIES

Paper: Close to my Heart
Scissors: Deckle edge, Fiskars
Stickers: Making Memories
Pen: Micron Pigma, Sakura
Milk bottle: Kim's own design
Idea to note: Kim created the cookies
by tracing circles from a template and
trimming with Deckle-edged scissors.

A kid'll eat the middle of an OREO ...

Milk

Madison

and save the chocolate cookie outside for last!

Happy Birthday Grandma

Birthday Sundae R·E·C·I·P·E

Directions

Begin with one scoop of **Michaela**. This is the foundation for any good birthday Sundae. A big scoop of Michaela ensures plenty of **Cuteness** & **Laughter** on your special day and holds the entire sundae together. Add to this a generous scoop of **Cameron**. Without the Cameron there will not be enough infectious **Giggles** which are completely necessary for a truly spectacular Sundae. Finally, garnish with one ripe **Raina** for extra sweetness. Ripeness is determined by the size of the dimple on the left cheek. The Raina will give your Sundae a **Zing**! You may wish to sprinkle a little **Mike** & **Gina** on top. They really only add pride to a Sundae they feel is already perfect!

Michaela, 1/97

Cameron, 1/97

"Birthday Sundae"

by Gina Bowers
Chandler, Arizona

SUPPLIES

Stickers: Mrs. Grossman's
Die cuts: Ellison
Pens: Zig Clean Color, EK Success
Circle cutter: Fiskars
Sundae glass: Gina's own design
Idea to note: Create a scrapbook page as
a special "birthday card" as Gina did for
Grandma's 72nd birthday!

"Mama Mia"

by Kim Cook
The Heartland Paper Co.
Bountiful, Utah

SUPPLIES

Paper: The Paper Patch; Carson Dellosa
Templates: Deja Views; Family Treasures

Mama Mia!

I love pizza!

"We've Got Cookies"

by Lezlye Lauterbach
Campbell, California

SUPPLIES

Paper: Close to my Heart
Letter stencil: Dream Talk, Close to my Heart
Die cut: Ellison
Pen: Micron Pigma, Sakura
Rubber stamp: D.O.T.S.
Idea to note: Lezlye cut pictures of each cookie out of the cookie packaging and included them on her layout.

"First Time Painting"

by Beth Pearson
Provo, Utah

SUPPLIES

Rubber stamps: Alphabet Attitude, Stampin' Up!
Wavy paint lines: Borderlines, Creative Memories
Paint brush: Beth's own design
Idea to note: Using stamped letters is easy and looks great! Use a wavy ruler for a great "flow" of color.

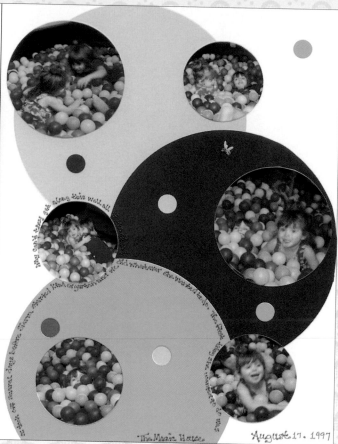

The beginning of our pre-Kindergarten spree.

The Magic House

August 17, 1997

"The Magic House"

by Angie McGoveran
Festus, Missouri

SUPPLIES

Sticker: Mrs. Grossman's
Circle cutter: Fiskars
Circle punch: Family Treasures
Pen: Zig Millennium, EK Success

AIR

RYAN

"Air Ryan"

by Stacy Smith
Lanham, Maryland

SUPPLIES

Scissors: Wave edge, Fiskars
Stickers: Creative Memories;
Mrs. Grossman's
Pens: Micron Pigma, Sakura
Hole punch: Gem, McGill
Basketball standard: Stacy's own design
Idea to note: Stacy used a hole punch to
create the basketball net.

"The Big Bug Hunt"

by Breneé Williams
Boise, Idaho

SUPPLIES

Paper: The Paper Patch
Scissors: Seagull edge, Fiskars
Stickers: Mrs. Grossman's
Pen: Micron Pigma, Sakura
Rubber stamps: Dream Talk, D.O.T.S.
Lady bug: Breneé's own design

"Mrs. Sarver's Nursery"

by Erin Garth
La Mesa, California

SUPPLIES

Punches: Gem, McGill; Family Treasures
Pen: LePlume, Marvy Uchida
Girl die cut: Erin's own design
Idea to note: Erin created the girl die cut
to mimic her daughter's outfit.

We had been waiting for weeks for the El Niño storms to pass so that we could take a drive up to the Sarver Nursery in San Marcos. On March 21, 1998 it was finally dry enough to go.

The Sarver Nursery is owned and operated by Rosalind Sarver, who at 92 raises over 75 varieties of canna lilies and azaleas. We were hoping to meet her but were told that she was taking a nap. We were happy to show ourselves around a small part of the 32 acre nursery. Lily found some empty pots and a potting table and decided to get to work. We came home just before the rains started again with eight canna lilies, and the promise to return in August when the lily fields would be in full bloom.

"Jumping the Day Away"

by Megan Staker
Provo, Utah

SUPPLIES

Paper: Colors By Design
Spiral punch: All Night Media
Daisy stationery: Mara-Mi
Pen: Zig Writer, EK Success

"Pizza Party"

by Angelyn Bryce
West Chester, Pennsylvania

SUPPLIES

Letter template: Frances Meyer
Pen: Zig Writer, EK Success

For Ricky's 7th birthday we went to see "The Borrowers" and then we came home for Pizza!

The kids had fun and it was easy on mom!

Our traditional chocolate chip pancake breakfast!

Yoko called me at the start of the year for advice about piano lessons for Jessica.

I contacted my former piano instructor, Mrs. Rejto, to request an interview appointment.

Mrs. Rejto and Jessica met and became instant friends. Mrs. Rejto decided to take Jessica as a student.

Mrs. Rejto and I have kept in touch over the years. However, it is truly a honor that our little flowergirl is receiving piano instruction under my favorite piano teacher.

As I sat in the audience listening to Jessica perform, it brought back so many fond memories of my own 18 years of classical piano training.

I hope that Jessica will enjoy the piano as much as I did and still do on occasion. Maybe Jessica and I can perform a duet next year!

Jessica's 1st piano recital...

Jessica patiently and nervously awaiting her turn at the piano.

Jessica made a new friend, a fellow classical pianist.

July 8, 1997
Sun., 4:00 p.m.
at the home of
Mrs. Alice Rejto
Beverly Hills, CA

Jessica flawlessly performed three compositions.

We dined at Jimmy's in Beverly Hills to celebrate afterwards.

"Jessica's Piano Recital"
by Yuko Neal
Huntington Beach, California
SUPPLIES
Scissors: Majestic edge, Fiskars
Sticker: Frances Meyer
Font: DJ Classic, Fontastic!, D.J. Inkers
Pen: Zig Writer, EK Success; Callipen, Sakura

"School Girl"
by Terina Darcey
Tulsa, Oklahoma
SUPPLIES
Scissors: Scallop and Clouds edges, Fiskars
Crimper: Fiskars
Other: Terina included a button on her page.

MOVING ON UP

Crossing the threshold from child to adult can be a little difficult as well as very exciting. Capture each milestone—from prom, to graduation, to marriage, anniversaries and careers. Covering adolescence to old age, this section will give you many ideas to help you preserve the highlights of your life.

"Gigi Does the Mall"
by Joyce Schweitzer
Greensboro, North Carolina

SUPPLIES
Paper: Creative Card Company
Die cuts: Accu-Cut Systems
Letter stickers: Creative Memories
Pens: Micron Pigma, Sakura; Zig Opaque Writer, EK Success
Star punches: Marvy Uchida; Family Treasures

August
1997

FDR Memorial
Korean War Memorial

THE STRUCTURE OF WORLD PEACE CANNOT BE THE WORK OF ONE MAN, OR ONE PARTY, OR ONE NATION... IT MUST BE A PEACE WHICH RESTS ON THE COOPERATIVE EFFORT OF THE WHOLE WORLD.

ELEANOR ROOSEVELT
FIRST UNITED STATES DELEGATE
TO THE UNITED NATIONS

Which war was this?

THEY (WHO) SEEK TO ESTABLISH SYSTEMS OF GOVERNMENT BASED ON THE REGIMENTATION OF ALL HUMAN BEINGS BY A HANDFUL OF INDIVIDUAL RULERS ... CALL THIS A NEW ORDER. IT IS NOT NEW AND IT IS NOT ORDER.

Crazy kind of zoo?

Scissors: Ripple edge by Fiskars.

"40th Anniversary"
by Colleen Adams
Huntington Beach, California

SUPPLIES

Pen: Zig Opaque Writer, EK Success;
Micron Pigma, Sakura
Stickers: Mrs. Grossman's
Die cuts: Accu-Cut Systems
Foil papers: Source unknown

"A Winning Hand"
by Debbie Sammons
Placentia, California

SUPPLIES

Letter stickers: Creative Memories
Idea to note: Debbie used a craft knife to cut
out the center of playing cards and then framed
her photos with the cards.

"Seeing Phantom"

by Megan Fowler
Memories By Design
Layton, Utah

SUPPLIES

Stickers: Mrs. Grossman's
Pen: Metallic Gelly Roll, Sakura
Idea to note: Megan incorporated elements of
the program to complete her page.

"At the Movies"

by Jackie Gravelle
Orem, Utah

SUPPLIES

Stickers: Frances Meyer; Stickopotamus
Letter template: Pebble Tracers, Pebbles in my Pocket
Cloud punch: Family Treasures
Idea to note: Jackie took a picture of the marquee and
included her ticket stubs—what a great way
to remember life's little moments. Jackie also
made "popcorn" with a small cloud punch.

March 21, 1998
We went to the movie with Janet and
Esdras. I brought my camera along to
take pictures for the Creating
Keepsakes scrapbook contest. I was
taking pictures of EVERYTHING. People
in the theatre must have thought I was
crazy. I know Esdras did. I didn't care.
I was having a BLAST!!! It was fun
playing around and creating pictures
that I knew I would stick die cuts in
later on. The guys had been wanting to
see "U.S. Marshalls," so Janet and I
agreed to go. Although the movie was a
little violent, we all gave it a big

Gary and Janet buying the movie tickets. The tickets cost $6.00 each.

"Engagement Pictures"
by Jane Nicolay
Fairway, Kansas
SUPPLIES
Stickers: Mrs. Grossman's
Pen: Micron Pigma, Sakura

"Best Friend's Wedding"
by Megan Fowler
Memories By Design
Layton, Utah
SUPPLIES
Stickers: Mrs. Grossman's
Letter stickers: Frances Meyer

Wedding date~June 6 '98

The future Mr. + Mrs. Schneider!

They got engaged on March 27!

Megan and Al's engagement pictures!

They got engaged in the park across from their house!

July 2

MY BEST FRIENDS WEDDING

Sarah and Todd Kap March 21, 1998

We have been best friends ever since we were five yrs old! It was so neat to see Sarah be the first one of all us friends to get married! We'll be Best Friends Forever!

Natalie and Sarah My two Best Friends

The Reception was held at the Heather Glen Ward. The place looked beautiful! All us girls just hung out until the very end when Sarah and Todd left for their Honeymoon to Las Vegas!

Bountiful Temple

An Evening to Remember

One day while Aunt Ivy was doing the crossword from the newspaper, she came across this article and thought it sounded interesting. Well, the following Monday evening we were having an unforgettable evening!

It was a game dinner and we were served a different wine with each course—and we had all five desserts! It was wonderful!

"An Evening to Remember"

by Pat Murray
Edmonton, Alberta, Canada

SUPPLIES

Stickers: The Gifted Line
Corner edger: Nostalgia edge, Fiskars
Pens: Zig Opaque Writer, EK Success
Mulberry paper: Personal Stamp Exchange
Idea to note: Consider using stickers for a fun corner embellishment.

"Wine Country"

by Sandy O'Donovan
Gilroy, California

SUPPLIES

Circle punches: McGill; Family Treasures
Hole punch: Punch Line, McGill
Pen: LePlume, Marvy Uchida
Idea to note: Use circle and hole punches to create your own cluster of grapes.

"50th Birthday"

by Joyce Schweitzer

Greensboro, North Carolina

SUPPLIES

Scissors: Scallop edge, Fiskars

Die cut: Accu-Cut Systems

Pens: Micron Pigma, Sakura; Zig Writer, EK Success

Grim Reaper: Joyce's own design

"Happy Birthday"

by Joyce Schweitzer

Greensboro, North Carolina

SUPPLIES

Stickers: Mrs. Grossman's; Creative Memories

Scissors: Bubbles and Seagull (corner) edges, Fiskars

Pens: Micron Pigma, Sakura

Die cuts: Accu-Cut Systems

April 1997

Terry misbehavin' again! (Wanda's series got delivered to Joyce...Oops!)

Door wreath from Susies.

Aunt Elizabeth amazed!

Birthday lunch at Pandowdy's.

50th Birthday

Relax...I'm just here for the cake!

HAPPY BIRTHDAY TO US!

August 1997

1997 brought six 50th Birthdays to celebrate – Terry & Norma Kingsbery; Bobby & Judy Deeter; Joyce & Wanda Hill

Over 100 friends waited at their home for a surprise!

"Sweet 16"
by Shellie Sepulveda
The Paper Attic
Sandy, Utah
SUPPLIES
Paper: The Paper Patch
Die cuts: Ellison

Juke box: Colors by Design
Scissors: Deckle edge, Fiskars
Pen: Zig Opaque Writer,
EK Success
Idea to note: Shellie used
different-sized circles to
create records.

"Toy Story"
by Karen Petersen
Mom and Me Scrapbooking
Salt Lake City, Utah
SUPPLIES
Die cuts: Accu-Cut Systems

"Chico State"

by Carolyn Klein
Tustin, California

SUPPLIES

Paper: Paper Pizazz,
Hot Off The Press
Sticker: Mrs. Grossman's

Scissors: Victorian edge, Fiskars
Computer clip art: Print Shop
Premier 5.0, Broderbund;
Art Explosion 40,000
Idea to note: Carolyn included
her daughter's essay on her lay-
out.

"Huskies"

by Vicki Garner
Memories By Design
Layton, Utah

SUPPLIES

Paper: Memory Press
Stickers: Frances Meyer
Letter template: Pebble Tracers, Pebbles in my Pocket
Other: Vicki cut the huskies out of a greeting card.

the Class of 1995

Trinity Christian Academy

Me, Susan Marks and Tracy Williamson

Grandpa and Grandma

Aunt Laura and Uncle Dave

Mom and me at the Senior Tea

I did it!

Jenny and Aaron Hershberger

Powder Puff Football

"Class of 1995"

by Deanna Furey
Jacksonville, Florida

SUPPLIES

Rubber stamp: Source unknown
Scissors: Deckle edge, Fiskars
Sticker: Source unknown

"Graduation Day"

by Roberta Rosenstein
Mount Vernon, Washington

SUPPLIES

Background drawing: by James R. Westling
Poem: by Roberta Rosenstein
Computer font: Amaze and Times New Roman
Idea to note: Illustrate the passage of time by
showing pictures of then and now.

GRANGER
Lancers

The 1995 Senior Class of Granger High School

Granger High School
Commencement Exercises
Abravanel Hall
June 6, 1995
4:00 p.m.

"Granger Lancers"
by Megan Staker
Provo, Utah

SUPPLIES
Pens: Zig Opaque Writer,
EK Success; Hybrid, Pentel
Idea to note: Megan included her
student ID, and a copy of her diploma
and commencement ticket.

"Chatfield Senior High Graduation"
by Megan Staker
Provo, Utah

SUPPLIES
Pen: Hybrid, Pentel
Scissors: Deckle edge, Family Treasures

chatfield senior high
graduation
AT
Red Rocks

"Friends Forever"

by Jennifer Keith
Memory Preserves
Burbank, California

SUPPLIES

Die cuts: Memory Preserves
Pen: Zig Writer, EK Success

"Future's So Bright"

by Vicki Garner
Memories By Design
Layton, Utah

SUPPLIES

Paper: The Paper Patch
Sun punch: Family Treasures
Paper-piecing pattern: Windows of Time
Computer font: DJ Salsa, Dazzle Daze, D.J. Inkers

"Friends"

by LeNae Gerig
Hot Off The Press
Canby, Oregon

SUPPLIES

Paper: Paper Pizazz, Hot Off The Press
Scissors: Ripply edge, McGill
Pen: Zig Writer, EK Success

"Rachel Rocks"

by Judy Hopkins
Valencia, California

SUPPLIES

Stickers: Frances Meyer; Mrs Grossman's
Letter stickers: Creative Memories

Star punch: Family Treasures
Die cuts: Ellison
Pen: Zig Writer, EK Success
Scissors: Bubbles edge, Fiskars;
Nostalgia edge, Creative Memories

"The Jog"

by Rebecca Coon
Iona, Idaho

SUPPLIES

Stickers: Frances Meyer
Die cuts: Accu-Cut Systems
Pen: Micron Pigma and Callipen, Sakura
Traffic signal: Rebecca's own design

"Skating Buddies"
by Megan Staker
Provo, Utah
SUPPLIES
Die cuts: Ellison
Pen: Zig Opaque Writer, EK Success
Metallic paper: Accu-Cut Systems

"Downtown Denver"
by Megan Staker
Provo, Utah
SUPPLIES
Corner template: Nuevo Corner Designs
Photo corners: Lineco
Idea to note: Megan created the column
with a craft knife.

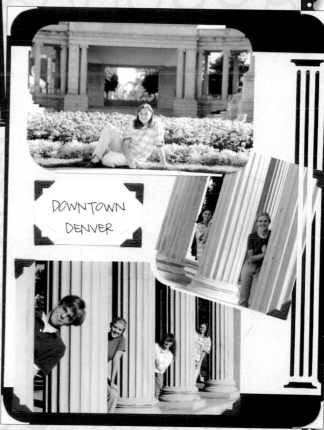

"The Open Road"
by Debi Boler
Newport Beach, California
SUPPLIES
Paper: The Paper Patch
Stickers: Mrs. Grossman's
Computer font: DJ Serif, Fontastic!,
D.J. Inkers

Die cuts: Pebbles in my Pocket;
Ellison
Scissors: Deckle edge, Fiskars
Pens: Zig Millennium, EK Success;
Pen Touch, Sakura
Song lyrics: "The Goofy Movie,"
Disney Productions

"My First Car"

by Christie Scott
Trevor, Wisconsin

SUPPLIES

Stickers: Frances Meyer
Colored pencils: Prisma Color, Berol
Mustang: Christie's own design

"Eric Is 16"

by Tammy Lutz
High Point, North Carolina

SUPPLIES

Pens: Micron Pigma, Sakura; Zig Opaque Writer, EK Success
Paper: Paper Pizazz, Hot Off The Press
Stickers: Making Memories

MY FIRST CAR

1969 MUSTANG

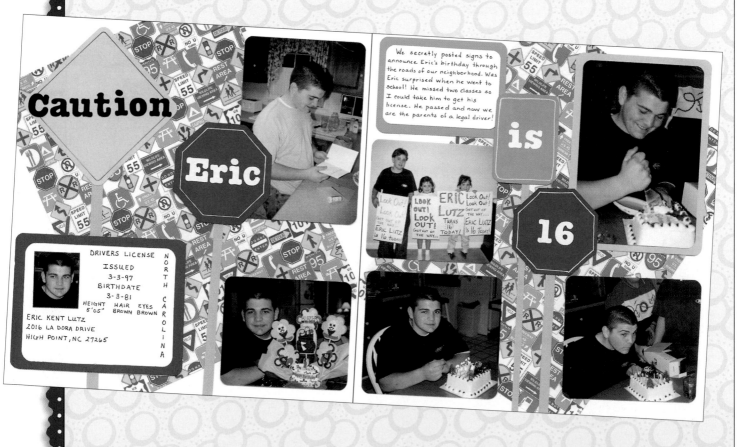

Caution

Eric is 16

We secretly posted signs to announce Eric's birthday through the roads of our neighborhood. Was Eric surprised when he went to school! He missed two classes so I could take him to get his license. He passed and now we are the parents of a legal driver!

DRIVERS LICENSE
ISSUED 3-3-97
BIRTHDATE 3-3-81
HEIGHT 5'05" HAIR BROWN EYES BROWN
ERIC KENT LUTZ
2016 LA DORA DRIVE
HIGH POINT, NC 27265
NORTH CAROLINA

Chad asked me to Prom, I can hardly wait. I want this to be the perfect date. So Mirror Mirror what do you see... Which one of these dresses was made just for me.

March 21, 1998

"Mirror, Mirror"

by Desiree Garner
Kaysville, Utah

SUPPLIES

Paper-piecing pattern: I Feel Pretty, Windows of Time
Computer font: Bookplate, Print Artist
Heart punch: Family Treasures
Idea to note: Desiree used circle punches to create miniature "flowers."

"Spring Ball"

by Nancy Geweke
Yuba City, California

SUPPLIES

Pen: Micron Pigma, Sakura
Scissors: Victorian edge, Fiskars
Die cuts: Ellison
Circle punches: Family Treasures; Marvy Uchida
Pen: Micron Pigma, Sakura
Other: Lace doily

March 21, 1998

Me, Ryan, Ernie and Joanne

What a great night! I went with Ryan Whitmer and Joanne went with Ernie Harris. We went to Pasquinis for dinner, came to our house and then off to the dance!

spring ball

"Ambulance"

by Donna Collins
Valencia, California
SUPPLIES
Pen: Zig Writer, EK Success
Ambulance: Donna's own design

"Emergency 911"

by Laurel Leonard
Tacoma, Washington
SUPPLIES
Paper: The Paper Patch
Stickers: Mrs. Grossman's; Frances Meyer
Die cuts: Ellison
Scissors: Peaks edge, Fiskars; Jumbo pinking edge, Family Treasures
Computer font: Times New Roman
Pen: Gelly Roll, Sakura

Kristin Serina is an Emergency Medical Technician and drives an ambulance. She was in our area and gave us a tour of her rig.

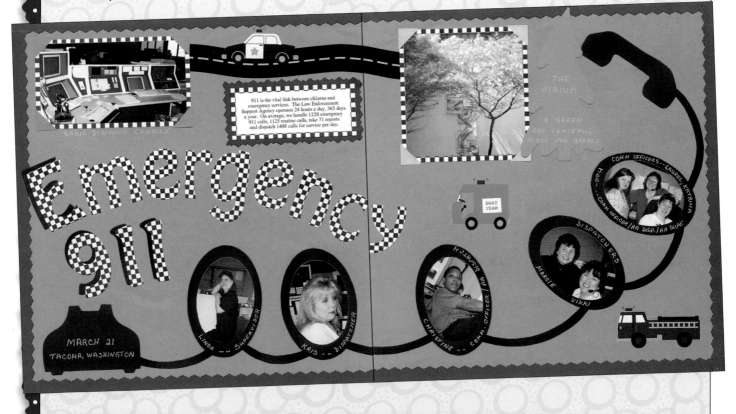

HOME

Before

Our house as it was in October 1993 when we bought it.

After

The house without a rocky front yard (we moved it all ourselves-- ugh) and with new landscaping by the walk. Dec. '96

IMPROVEMENTS

Our bedroom before "renovations"

Let's paint the walls Chris gets started

New paint, new comforter. We're all set!

June 1996

Chris hated the vinyl floor in the kitchen. So, together Mark & Chris tore up the old floor. It took quite awhile to do. We had to use an iron on a wet towel to heat each vinyl square in order to loosen the glue. A real pain, but look at the new tile we installed instead... gorgeous! May-November, 1996

"Home Improvements"

by Chris Suchanek
Austin, Texas

SUPPLIES

Cloud stamp: Visual Image Printery
Stamp pad: ColorBox, Clearsnap, Inc.
Stickers: Mrs. Grossman's; Frances Meyer; Creative Memories
Pens: Micron Pigma, Sakura
Colored pencils: Crayola

grandpa Lowry 1998

"Grandpa Lowry"

by Megan Staker
Provo, Utah

SUPPLIES

Paper: The Paper Patch; Paper Pizazz, Hot Off The Press
Horseshoe die cuts: Ellison
Pens: Zig Opaque Writer, EK Success
Photo corners: Stampington Co.

Tanners haircut

Snip - Snip - opps!

Reattaching the Ear!

Buzz! Now what are you doin?

Are you done yet?

Curls and Chickee Feathers

remnants

Mommy says…

1st

talking on the phone & pay attention to me.

I'm handsome.

Aug. 7, 1997

"Tanner's First Haircut"
by Vangie Norton
Mesa, Arizona
SUPPLIES
Die cuts: Ellison
Letter template: Frances Meyer
Pens: Pentel; Zig Writer, EK Success
Barber poles: Vangie's own design
Idea to note: Vangie cut strips of cardstock to create the stripes on the barber poles. She also included a piece of Tanner's hair.

WHAT A BABE

A baby feels so soft and cuddly in

your arms. And there's nothing

more delightful than when your baby

begins to giggle and coo. This is a

precious time of life, so be sure to

preserve your baby's first year with

all of the great ideas found in this

section. From taking that first step to

your baby's first haircut, this section

has you covered.

"Cody Cooper, Age 2"

by Katherine Ware
Magna, Utah

SUPPLIES

Paper: Paper Pizazz, Hot Off The Press
Stickers: Frances Meyer
Ink spots: Blitzer, EK Success

"Joshua Holverson"

by Jewelene Holverson
Pocatello, Idaho

SUPPLIES

Scissors: Bubbles edge, Fiskars
Pen: Micron Pigma, Sakura
Punches: McGill (jumbo heart);
Carl (jumbo star, small circle)

"Rachel"

by Carole Kamradt
The Paper Attic
Sandy, Utah

SUPPLIES

Flower paper: Frances Meyer
Pink paper: Close to my Heart
Scissors: Jumbo Scallop edge, Fiskars
Pens: Zig Millennium, EK Success
Punch: Micro Punch, McGill

"Zane Pedersen"

by Jenni McBride
Memories By Design
Layton, Utah

SUPPLIES
Stickers: Mrs. Grossman's
Rubber stamp: Imaginations
Idea to note: Jenni created her own background paper with a rubber stamp.

"Caleb's Turning 1"

by Kelly Clauss
Yorba Linda, California

SUPPLIES
Rubber stamp: D.O.T.S.
Paper: The Paper Patch
Greeting card: Greeting Graphics
Candle: Azadi Earles
Stickers: Frances Meyer
Idea to note: Kelly included a copy of the birthday invitation, complete with blue ribbon.

"Pooh Party"

by Tawnya Rhode
West Linn, Oregon
SUPPLIES
Scissors: Seagull and Bubbles
edges, Fiskars
Stickers: Sandylion; Mrs. Grossman's
Winnie the Pooh: Traced from
a "Pooh" book

"Happy Birthday to Me"
by Tawnya Rhode
West Linn, Oregon
SUPPLIES
Scissors: Colonial edge, Fiskars
Stickers: Disney; Mrs. Grossman's

"A Walk through My 1st Year"
by Deb Day
Coon Rapids, Minnesota
SUPPLIES
Letter stickers: Creative Memories
Die cuts: Source unknown
Paper: The Paper Patch

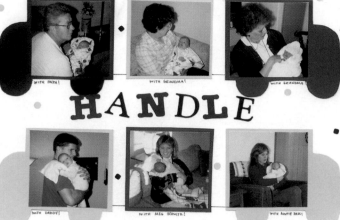

"Handle with Care"

by Deb Day
Coon Rapids, Minnesota

SUPPLIES

Stickers: Creative Memories
Pen: Micron Pigma, Sakura
Trucks: Deb's own design

"Cutest Boy in the Solar System"

by Laura Thompson
Spanish Fork, Utah

SUPPLIES

Stickers: Mrs. Grossman's
Die cuts: Ellison

"Just Like Daddy"

by Kelly Clauss
Yorba Linda, California

SUPPLIES

Computer font: DJ Fat Chat, Fontastic!, D.J. Inkers
Paper: The Paper Patch
Stickers: Stickopotamus
Pen: LePlume, Marvy Uchida

The Many Faces Of Jeffrey...

1. Jeffrey loves to play in the bathtub. He would sit and kick his legs until the water got to cold.

2. Jeffrey was excited the first night we put him to go to sleep in his new bed. That didn't last for long because he figured out that mommy & daddy left when he was in there.

3. Jeffrey loves to lay on the floor and roll around. It gives him a little bit of indepence.

4. Isn't He So Cute!

5. Jeffrey is quite the little Old Navy model. He dresses better than his mommy & daddy.

6. Jeffrey and James received matching ties for Christmas one year. James loved it. They make such a great team.

7. Jeffrey is always so happy. He rarely ever cries. The smile is pretty much a permanet fixture on his face.

8. The is Jeffrey's "I am so excited for whatever is coming" face.

"The Many Faces of Jeffrey"

by Jenni McBride
Memories By Design
Layton, Utah

SUPPLIES

Bear punch: Family Treasures
Paper: The Paper Patch

"Maxwell Davis Rank"

by Michele Rank
Torrance, California

SUPPLIES

Paper: D.O.T.S.
Pens: Dual Tip, Tombow
Stamps: D.O.T.S.
Scissors: Deckle edge, Family Treasures
Font: DJ Crayon, Fontastic!, D.J. Inkers
Idea to note: Don't forget to include special memories, stories and personality traits in your scrapbook.

Maxwell Davis Rank

Our youngest son, born 6/7/96. Your labor was induced by your mom's persistence pleas to her doctor. You were born healthy and as the nurse put 1" the largest head she had ever measured". We now know that your head was large to accommodate your individualsty which we now know as the "Maxinator". Just foreshadowing for things to come. This would be apparent soon after you came home. This would be brother Zachary just sixteen months older than you. Still very much a baby himself. Now our family has four members just the way your mommy and daddy had planned. Since you are the second child we really did not have to learn how to be parents just how to juggle two children's needs at one time. Your older brother was fascinated by you, and only the occasional outburst of jealousy. Overall we all coped well with our new little blessed child. As a infant you loved brightly colored toys. Your favorite were balls and anything else you could throw. Just like your brother you loved the swing and bouncer. I will never forget how you would put your hand out to stop the swinging motion on the swing. Or how in the bouncer you would throw the toys down just to have mommy put them back in the tray for you. Oh what joy you had making me keep you happy. I still miss the closeness we had when I would breast feed you. It was time for just Max and mommy. I look back and cherish those moments alone with you. Your parents developed a special place in our hearts for your youngest son. As soon as you became mobile our simple days were finished. You developed much faster than your brother. You crossed the steps of babyhood on average three months sooner than your brother. Standing, Crawling and walking were easy obstacles to you. Nothing seems to slow you down. Now you started to make your brothers life more difficult. Anything brother had you would make a personal goal to take from him. This would cause major trauma in Zachary's life. Zach learned fast that hitting, biting, pushing and poking were not acceptable solutions to dealing with you. Things have calmed down now that you are almost two years old. The brothers finally play together. We still have battles and hurt feelings to deal with, but all in all you two now enjoy each other. What joy we have in seeing our two boys playing side by side with your hot wheels our lego blocks. So, Maxwell you will always be our little bundle of joy, our youngest son. All our love now and forever.

Love, Mommy and Daddy
4/16/96

11 Months

Every cabinet
was locked
except the pots
& pans and one
drawer. What a
time Amy had
in the kitchen!

Amy & Daddy were inseparable.
She was always so excited when
he got home because that meant
"party time"!

Amy loved to empty the basket
of toys by throwing them one-
by-one and then she was done.

"All Aboard for a Busy Day"

by Debbie Meyer
Elida, Ohio

SUPPLIES
Stickers: Mrs. Grossman's
Heart punch: Marvy Uchida
Die cuts: Ellison; Creative Memories
Rub-ons: Magic Memories, Chartpak

"Grandpa Darryl & Megan"

by Sherrie Barker
Perry, Utah

SUPPLIES
Leaf stamp: Source unknown

July 1997
Grandpa Darryl
made   tire swing
for the swingset.

Kristen is holding
Megan. I can
really see Jordan,
Megan's Aunt in
gan in these pic-
tures.
Megan is wearing
the first out fit that
Ashley & I made for
er. We sewed quite
a few out fits
together.

Grandpa Darryl and Megan July-
August 1997, babysitting on Friday's while Melissa goes to work
and cleans houses.
Notice the chubby in above picture, it's Darryl's latest, cottage
cheese, salsa and sour cream.
In the hammock, Megan has to
share Grandpa Darryl with Beauty
too.
Megan has always loved to be outside. She likes to watch the mov-
ing leaves when the wind is blowing. She has really enjoyed the
hammock. Darryl made and hung
the hammock this past spring.
Sharaya Shaw left Ashley the horse
to use when she babysat and
Megan really seems to enjoy it.

"Cover Girl"

by Jennifer Wright
Lafayette, Indiana

SUPPLIES

Paper: The Paper Patch
Stickers: Stickopotamus
Scissors: Pinking edge, Fiskars
Punches: Marvy Uchida
(circle, foot)

Die cut: Ellison
Computer clip art: Click Art,
Rogerman
Idea to note: Jennifer made
"cotton balls" with a circle punch,
then placed them between the
toes on the foot die cuts.

"Chicken Pops"

by Stacy March
Cocoa, Florida

SUPPLIES

Clip art: Spring Wing Dings, D.J. Inkers
Paper: D.O.T.S.
Letter template: Frances Meyer
Pen: Micron Pigma, Sakura
Scissors: Scallop edge, Fiskars

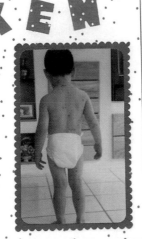

The First 12 Months

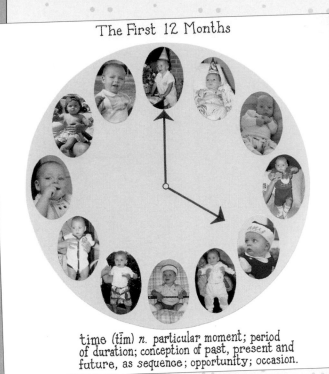

time (tĭm) *n.* particular moment; period of duration; conception of past, present and future, as sequence; opportunity; occasion.

Photos by J.J Hollis at 1 month old

"The First 12 Months"

by Anita Ochab
Orlando, Florida
SUPPLIES
Pens: Zig Millennium, EK Success
Die cuts: Scrappers

"Ryan's GeeGee Blankie"

by Ali Johnson
D.J. Inkers
Springville, Utah
SUPPLIES
Stickers: D.J. Inkers
Computer font: DJ Crazed, Fontastic! 2, D.J. Inkers
Idea to note: Ali color-copied her son's blanket and included it on her scrapbook page.

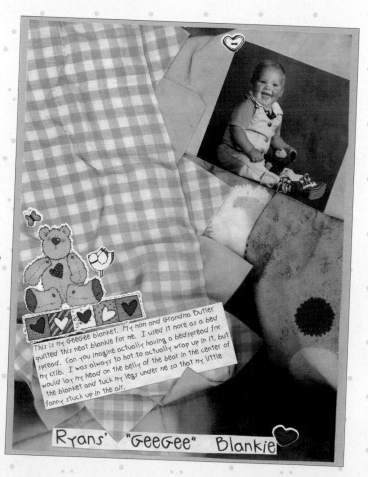

This is my GeeGee blanket. My mom and Grandma Butler quilted this neat blankie for me. I used it here as a bed spread. Can you imagine actually having a bedspread for my crib. I was always to hot to actually wrap up in it, but would lay my head on the belly of the bear in the center of the blanket and tuck my legs under me so that my little fanny stuck up in the air.

Ryans' "GeeGee" Blankie

"Fun in the Sun with Andrea"

by Pat Murray
Edmonton, Alberta, Canada

SUPPLIES

Stickers: Stickopotamus
Die cut: Ellison
Paper: The Paper Patch
Pens: LePlume, Marvy Uchida

"Fun in the Sun with Rachel"

by Pat Murray
Edmonton, Alberta, Canada

SUPPLIES

Scissors: Pinking edge, Fiskars
Paper: The Paper Patch; NRN Designs
Stickers: The Gifted Line
Die cut: Ellison

"Bubbles"

by Jodi Olson
Kaysville, Utah

SUPPLIES

Paper: Paper Pizazz,
Hot Off The Press
Scissors: Clouds edge, Fiskars
Circle cutter: Fiskars
Template: Provo Craft
Pens: Zig Writer, EK Success

"Playing in the Leaves"

by Jodi Olson
Kaysville, Utah

SUPPLIES

Scissors: Leaf edge, Fiskars
Die cut: Ellison
Pen: Micron Pigma, Sakura
Idea to note: Jodi used
the Leaf-edge scissors to
create a jagged border
around her page.

"It's Cold Out Baby"

by Pat Murray
Edmonton, Alberta, Canada

SUPPLIES

Paper: The Paper Patch
Rub-ons: First Impressions,
Provo Craft
Pens: Zig Clean Color,
EK Success

"Shh ... Baby's Sleeping"

by Linda Beeson
Ventura, California
SUPPLIES
Paper: Northern Spy; The Paper Patch
Scissors: Pinking and Bubbles edges, Fiskars;
Jumbo Scallop edge, Family Treasures
Stickers: Making Memories
Templates: Provo Craft
Stamps: Stamps by Judith
Ink: Memories
Pens: LePlume, Marvy Uchida; Gelly Roll, Sakura

"Here Comes the Sandman"

by Teresa Lewis
Sandy, Utah
SUPPLIES
Font: DJ Fancy, Fontastic!, D.J. Inkers
Idea to note: Teresa found this paper in a children's book
(*Susanna and the Sandman* by Monika Laimgruber,
North-South Books, New York).

"Atta Boy"

by Shellie Sepulveda
The Paper Attic
Sandy, Utah
SUPPLIES
Paper: Frances Meyer
Scissors: Deckle edge, Fiskars
Stickers: Frances Meyer

"I Could Live in My Underwear"

by Lynne Hansen
Moore, South Carolina
SUPPLIES
Paper: The Paper Patch
Letter stickers: Source unknown
Punches: Family Treasures (heart, star)
Underwear: Lynne's own design

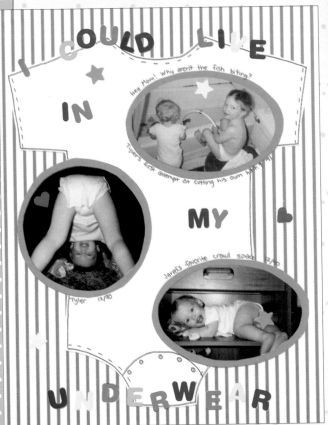

"What a Big Girl"

by Carole Kamradt
The Paper Attic
Sandy, Utah
SUPPLIES
Paper: The Paper Patch
Scissors: Mini-Pinking edge, Fiskars
Stickers: Frances Meyer
Pens: Gelly Roll, Sakura

"Katie Is Blossoming"

by Stephanie Barnard
Laguna Niguel, California

SUPPLIES

Scissors: Clouds edge, Fiskars
Stickers: Creative Memories
Die cut: Accu-Cut Systems

"Little People"

by Karen Petersen
Mom and Me Scrapbooking
Salt Lake City, Utah

SUPPLIES

Scissors: Scallop edge, Fiskars
Circle punch: Family Treasures
Little people: Karen's own design

"Quinton"

by Kristine Cline
Yakima, Washington

SUPPLIES

Paper: Creative Memories
Circle cutter: Creative Memories
Pens: Zig Opaque Writer, EK Success

Our Favorite Boy

QUINTON

Daddy taught Quinton how to twist an Oreo!

Always eat the middle first.

"Hot Diggidy Dog"

by Kiresten Harrison
Mesa, Arizona

SUPPLIES

Paper: The Paper Patch
Letter stickers: Making Memories
Hot dogs: Kiresten's own design

hot diggidy dog

"Uh-Oh, Spaghetti O's"

by Carol Laub
The Paper Attic
Sandy, Utah

SUPPLIES

Punches: Family Treasures
Die cuts: Ellison
Idea to note: Using different-sized circle punches, Carol created her own "Spaghetti O's." Carol also included a product label on the page.

uh oh

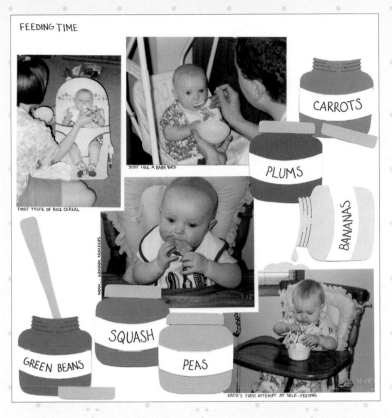

FEEDING TIME

FIRST TASTE OF RICE CEREAL

JUST LIKE A BABY BIRD

MMM... GRAHAM CRACKERS

CARROTS

PLUMS

BANANAS

GREEN BEANS

SQUASH

PEAS

KATIE'S FIRST ATTEMPT AT SELF-FEEDING

"Feeding Time"

by Tamra Dumolt
Oregon City, Oregon

SUPPLIES

Pens: Micron Pigma, Sakura

Jars: Tamra's own design

"Tyler's First Steps"

by Tawna Hansen
Vauxhall, Alberta, Canada

SUPPLIES

Paper: The Paper Patch

Scissors: Bow Tie edge, Fiskars

Stickers: Suzy's Zoo

Foot punch: Marvy Uchida

Idea to note: Tawna utilized the principle of repetition by taking an element from the photos (the kite) and reproducing it on her page.

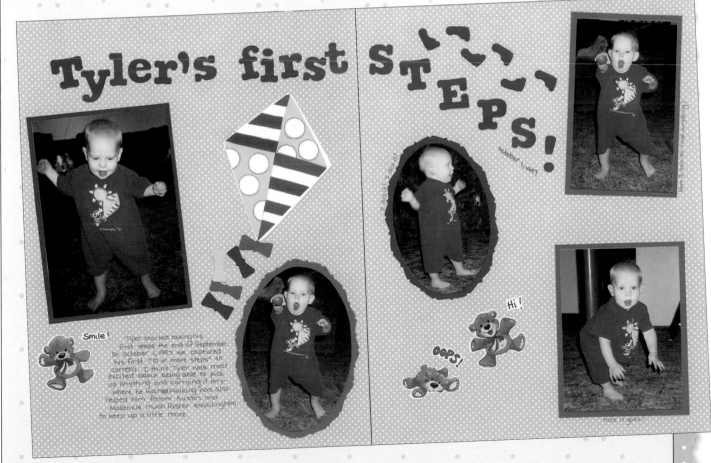

Tyler's first STEPS!

october 1, 1997

Smile!

Tyler started taking his first steps the end of September. On October 1, 1997 we captured his first "10 or more steps" on camera. I think Tyler was most excited about being able to pick up anything and carrying it anywhere he wanted. Walking has also helped him follow Austin and Makenzie much faster enabling him to keep up a little more.

Hi!

OOPS!

FESTIVE PHOTOS

A light snow begins to fall as

Christmas carolers come calling to

your door. The tree is glowing with

muted red and gold lights, and the

spicy scent of cinnamon and cloves

floats through the house. In this

section, we'll show you some great

ideas for preserving your family

traditions while making the spirit of

the season last all year long.

Scissors: Sunflower edge by Fiskars.

"Merry Christmas"

by Lisle Steelsmith
Bellevue, Washington

SUPPLIES

Paper: Paper Pizazz, Hot Off The Press; The Paper Patch

Stickers: Mrs. Grossman's; Creative Memories; Frances Meyer

Scissors: Seagull and Victorian edges, Fiskars

Templates: Creative Memories

Pens: Zig Opaque Writer, EK Success; Callipen, Sakura

Mom got a 10 minute giggle.

1997

Each of us is wearing another Christmas outfit and we are toasting the New Year with Code.

"Happy New Year"
by Joyce Schweitzer
Greensboro, North Carolina
SUPPLIES
Stickers: Mrs. Grossman's; Creative Memories
Scissors: Jumbo Pinking edge, Family Treasures;
Seagull edge (corner), Fiskars
Pen: Micron Pigma, Sakura

"Friends 1996"
by Jane Nicolay
Fairway, Kansas
SUPPLIES
Paper: Creative Memories
Stickers: Creative Memories; Mrs. Grossman's
Pens: Micron Pigma, Sakura
Scissors: Volcano edge, Fiskars

Brian, Michelle + Ethan (2) Kemp

Austin (4) + Brad (1) Collins

Anna + Caroline (1) Coleman

1996

Brian Spann (2)

FRIENDS

Katelyn (4), Kathleen (2) + Ashley (8) Devine

Jonathan (4) Mary K. Benjamin (2) + Greg Clinton

(4) Sajel, Tanis, Taber, Shalem Spani

Eddie (3) Shannon (2) + Megan (1) O'Mara

Connor (6) and Kyle (3) Manning

Sarah (2) Emily (9 mo) + Victoria (3) Godfrey

Boger

Zoe, Jack and Olivia

The Redfords - Rindi, Maddi, Rick, Lisa, Adam and Kiri

The Van Slootens - Erica, John, Nancy and Steven

Bill, Jan, Will, Joe Bevins

CHRISTMAS CARD PHOTOS

"Family Portraits"
by Nanci A. Kinser
Marietta, Georgia

SUPPLIES
Paper: Creative Memories
Stickers: Provo Craft; Creative Memories
Scissors: Deckle edge, Fiskars
Die cuts: Creative Memories
Idea to note: Cindy Wheeler of Marietta, Georgia, created the half-circle opening to the pocket page with her circle cutter.

"Here We Come A'Caroling"
by Marsha Peacock
Jacksonville, Florida

SUPPLIES
Stickers: Mrs. Grossman's; Creative Memories
Die cuts: Ellison
Pen: Micron Pigma, Sakura
Idea to note: Marsha offset the letter stickers with another color to create a shadowed effect (see "caroling").

HERE WE COME A CAROLING

Christmas Eve with my family: Dad, mom, Mitch, Benetta, Steven, David, mike, &yours Melanie

Melanie had a bad cold but still enjoyed all the festivities

After opening the presents we all gathered to sing Christmas carols. Dad played the vibraphone while mike played the piano.

The kids played the tambourine, bongo drums and sang on the microphone while mike "tickled the ivories".

Dad and mom have also given us wonderful christmas'.

Our Family's 1997 Christmas Card Portrait

This year Christmas was a combination of old and new. It was the first year we performed a family nativity play. Elise, of course, was Mary, Bryce was a shepherd, Marc was all 3 Wisemen, Collin was Joseph, Eric was resplendent as the Heavenly Host and Evan was a convincing donkey. We opened the traditional Christmas Eve Jammies, and Santa was good to everyone. We love being together!

"1997 Christmas Card Portrait"

by Catherine Allan
Twin Falls, Idaho

SUPPLIES

Scissors: Heartbeat edge, Fiskars
Stickers: Provo Craft
Punches: Family Treasures
Pen: Micron Pigma, Sakura
Idea to note: Make ornaments with your craft punches, then add doodles with a pen.

"Dear Santa"

by Janie Thomas
Blakely, Georgia

SUPPLIES

Paper: Creative Memories
Stickers: Hambly; Stickopotamus;
Creative Memories; Mrs. Grossman's
Pen: Zig Opaque Writer; EK Success
Newspaper: Early County News,
Blakely, Georgia

DEAR SANTA

North Pole News

December 25, 1997

Katlyn's hands and footprint at age 3 in December '96

Katlyn having a tea party with her cane bean!!

Showing off her bow from Diane Schafer-Katlyn just loved it!

Unwrapping a present from Santa Claus

Katlyn loved her Sit 'n Spin - she spun herself to death that day!!

"Katlyn's Hands"

by Rachel Leshko
Barron, Wisconsin

SUPPLIES

Paper: Creative Memories
Pen: Micron Pigma, Sakura
Idea to note: Rachel traced her daughter's handprints and one footprint to create the reindeer (idea inspired by Creative Memories).

"Christmas Eve at the Leishmans'"

by Marci Leishman
Draper, Utah

SUPPLIES

Paper: Paper Pizazz, Hot Off The Press; DMD Industries
Template: Provo Craft
Pen: Zig Writer, EK Success

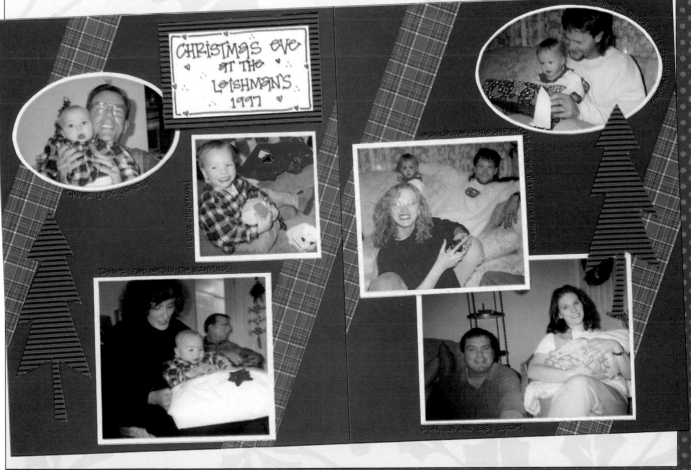

HERE I COME DOWN THE HILL

TYLER PLAYING IN SNOW AT OUR CABIN
IN WINTERPARK COLORADO
CHRISTMAS 1997

BEHIND HIS FORT!!!!

SNOWFLAKES AND LITTLE BOYS.
THERE ARE NO TWO ALIKE..

"Winter Park, Colorado"

by Rosemary Hines
Westminster, Colorado

SUPPLIES

Scissors: Ripple and Deckle edges, Fiskars
Stickers: Mrs. Grossman's
Die cuts: All My Memories

"Christmas Eve"

by Marci Leishman
Draper, Utah

SUPPLIES

Paper: The Paper Patch
Stickers: RA Lang
Gold pen: Marvy Uchida

CHRISTMAS EVE 1997

Kayden and Tanner looked so cute in their Christmas pajamas! We got a big surprise when Santa Claus came to our door! Santa wanted to make sure the boys were ready for bed so he could take care of business. Kayden and Tanner left him white chocolate macadamia nut cookies to snack on.

"We Have Been So Good"

by Vicki Garner
Memories By Design
Layton, Utah

SUPPLIES
Paper: The Paper Patch
Santa paper-piecing pattern: Windows of Time

"Christmas 1997"

by Marci Leishman
Draper, Utah

SUPPLIES
Paper: DMD Industries
Stickers: Making Memories
Templates: Provo Craft
Pen: Zig Writer, EK Success

Grandpa Hunt and Tanner sharing some bonding time.

Justin — "PEACE"

Jen and Kayden

Kayden was spoiled for Christmas!

Greg, Heather and Austin came to visit from New Mexico.

Heather and Austin

CHRISTMAS 1996

Christmas 1996 began with a fabulous music program at Haws. Casey and his schoolmates put on a great show. We spent Christmas with G.G and Papa in Rancho Cordova with a special side-trip to Gilroy to see Bev, Tina, Benjamin and Alexander.

"Rudolph the Red Nosed Reindeer"

Casey, Adam, Emilia, Chase Feddersen, Ben Stone and Cody Davis, all age 8.

"We Wish you a Merry Christmas"

Alexander gets a grip on Casey

Casey, Charlie & Alexander

Casey checks out his stocking

Casey with Papa & G.G's tree.

Charlie

"Christmas 1996"

by Colleen Adams
Huntington Beach, California

SUPPLIES

Paper: The Paper Patch
Letter stickers: Making Memories
Hole punch (⅛"): Punch Line, McGill
Pens: Zig Opaque Writer, EK Success
Die cuts: Ellison

"Friends and Family"

by Marci Leishman
Draper, Utah

SUPPLIES

Clip art: Holly Days, D.J. Inkers
Computer font: DJ Doodlers,
Fontastic!, D.J. Inkers
Scissors: Bow Tie edge, Fiskars
Pen: Zig Writer, EK Success

Merry Christmas friends & family

Sending you Christmas Wishes!

ENJOY the SEASON!

Love & From:
Robb, Marci, Kayden & Tanner Leishman

We sent this card and letter to everyone we know! Everyone thought that Kayden and Tanner looked just alike in the picture we sent. Maybe it was just the matching outfits!

"Cookie Fun"

by Wendy Smedley
Bountiful, Utah

SUPPLIES
Paper: The Paper Patch
Stationery: Frances Meyer
Scissors: Deckle edge, Fiskars
Stickers: Frances Meyer

Idea to note: Wendy cut out the gingerbread men from a piece of Frances Meyer Christmas stationery.

"Cookie Houses"

by Kristyn Hansen
Clearfield, Utah
SUPPLIES
Scissors: Shortblade and Small Wave edges, Family Treasures
Stickers: Mrs. Grossman's
Computer font: Kristyn downloaded this font from the Internet.
Pens: Zig Writer, EK Success
Gingerbread house: Kristyn's own design

Preston got all kinds of wonderful gifts. He un-wrapped games, cool T-shirts, art supplies, money from Granny and Papa, and much more!

"Christmas 1996"
by Kelli Collins
Mesa, Arizona
SUPPLIES
Paper: Sonburn; Paper Pizazz, Hot Off The Press
Stickers: Provo Craft
Pen: Zig Writer, EK Success

"Oh Little Town of Bethlehem"
by Jenny Jackson
Arlington, Virginia
SUPPLIES
Die cuts: Ellison
Star punch: Marvy Uchida
Pen: Zig Writer, EK Success

Oh Little Town of Bethlehem...

Christmas Eve 1996

You'd better not Pout !

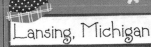
Christmas 1997

Yipeee! Barbie Bubbles! Exactly what I wanted..Thank you Santa! Raini asked Santa for only two things this year, & she got them both.

On Christmas Eve we let Raini open one present. She was so excited for a new computer game. This was the gift Gramma & Grampa Weller got for her, Jumpstart Preschool. Above, Raini holds a present in her Christmas dress.

Lansing, Michigan

The other thing she wanted was a grocery cart, & she got that, too. Here Raini shows off her new Christmas dress dancing in front of our Christmas tree.

Christmas '87

This Christmas we went to Buffalo Creek, Colorado to spend the holidays with Uncle Dave, Aunt Jackie, & James. Uncle Dave & Daddy made this cool looking Snowman... check him out !!

"You'd Better Not Pout"

by Emily Waters
East Lansing, Michigan
SUPPLIES
Paper: The Paper Patch; Northern Spy
Computer font: DJ FiddleSticks, FiddleSticks, D.J. Inkers
Craft punches: Marvy Uchida (snowflake); Punch Line, McGill (flower); Family Treasures (circle, heart)
Letter template: Pebble Tracers, Pebbles in my Pocket
Idea to note: Emily cut a heart punch out to make a mitten shape. She also used the circle punch to create part of the hats and topped them with the small flower punch.

"Christmas '87"

by Kelli Collins
Mesa, Arizona
SUPPLIES
Craft punches: Family Treasures
Paper: Provo Craft
Pens: Zig Writer, EK Success; Pentel
Snowman: Kelli's own design

One Sunday, we were actually ready for church a few minutes early & took the opportunity to take our family picture to put in our Christmas cards this year. It's one of the best pictures we have ever had taken & all we did was set the camera on the table & say Cheese!

"Family Portrait"

by Jenny Jackson
Arlington, Virginia

SUPPLIES

Paper: The Paper Patch
Craft punches: Family Treasures
Computer font: DJ Dash, Fontastic!, D.J. Inkers

"A Visit to Granny & Papa's"

by Kelli Collins
Mesa, Arizona

SUPPLIES

Paper: NRN Designs
Pens: Pilot; Zig Writer, EK Success
Ornaments and branch: Kelli's own design

"Christmas Reindeer"
by Vicki Garner
Memories By Design
Layton, Utah
SUPPLIES
Paper: The Paper Patch
Reindeer paper-piecing pattern: Windows of Time

What do you call Children who are afraid of Santa Claus?

Claustrophobic!!

"Claustrophobic"
by Janae Goerz
Maple Grove, Minnesota
SUPPLIES
Computer font: DJ Holly, Holly Days, D.J. Inkers
Craft punches: Family Treasures
Stickers: Mrs. Grossman's
Gold pen: Pentel

"Tanner and Kayden"
by Marci Leishman
Draper, Utah
SUPPLIES
Embossing template: Lasting Impressions for Paper

98 NCAA
NAL FOUR
MIFINALS

RDAY, MARCH 28, 1998
THE ALAMODOME
AN ANTONIO, TEXAS

LOWER LEVEL $50.00

138   29   18
SECTION ROW   SEAT

ENTER NORTH GATE
NO REFUNDS OR EXCHANGES

1998 NCAA
FINAL FOUR
CHAMPIONSHIP

MONDAY, MARCH 30, 1998
THE ALAMODOME
SAN ANTONIO, TEXAS

LOWER LEVEL $50.00

138   29   18
SECTION ROW   SEAT

ENTER NORTH GATE
NO REFUNDS OR EXCHANGES

1998 NCAA
Goin' to
Kansas City
WOMEN'S
FINAL FOUR

TELLING US ALL ABOUT IT! David and Dad went to the FINAL FOUR in San Antonio, Texas! They were gone 5 days, had a great time and in the semi-finals saw Utah beat North Carolina and Kentucky beat Stanford. They sure were the envy of lots of people here in Utah, but David is a true blue North Carolina fan. In the finals they saw KENTUCKY beat Utah for the National Championship!

At HOOP CITY there are lots of different basketball activities to try. David got some tips & an autograph from Jim Harrick, the Rhode Island coach!

Final Four® Memories f

THE ACTIVE LIFE

The blood's pumping, your muscles are

burning and the competition is fierce—

no, we're not talking about the business

world, this is sports at its best. From

highly competitive team sports to

putting around on the greens, there's

no doubt about it, today's lifestyle is an

active one. So peruse these page

layouts—you're sure to find ideas to

record your favorite pastime.

"Basketball Fan"
by Christie Lewis
Provo, Utah
SUPPLIES
Paper: Paper Pizazz, Hot Off The Press
Idea to note: Christie included ticket stubs and the
coach's signature from the basketball game.

BOX ELDER
BEES

Brent Hollingsworth
Ryan Brinkerhoff
Seth Putnam
Paul Walker
Brian Cusick
Greg Gunn
Ryan Hunsaker
Tyler Gilbert
Josh Harper
(bottom to top, left to right)

1997-98
SEASON

Zenoch Bishop
Jarom Bishop
Keith Mecham
Aaron Davis
Tyler Shaw
Derrek Tyler
Justin Simkins
Cody Blacker

(Bottom to top, left to right)

"Box Elder Bees"

by Sherrie Barker
Perry, Utah

SUPPLIES

Basketball stamp: Source unknown
Pen: Zig Writer, EK Success
Idea to note: By cropping the photos,
Sherrie put together a great team.

"Shooting Stars"

by Traci Johnson
Mesa, Arizona

SUPPLIES

Die cuts: Ellison
Paper: The Paper Patch
Pen: Zig Writer, EK Success
Idea to note: Traci created her
own basketball "o's" with a
circle punch and a pen.

"Skateboarding Rules"

by Christie Scott
Trevor, Wisconsin

SUPPLIES

Colored pencils: Prisma Color, Berol
Stickers: Mrs. Grossman's
Cloud template: Make an Impression
Stamp pad: ColorBox, Clearsnap, Inc.
Pen: Micron Pigma, Sakura
Skateboard ramp: Christie's own design

"Andy's Obsession"

by Andy Gottron
Hollister, California

SUPPLIES

Pens: Zig Writer, EK Success
Computer font: Times New Roman
Stickers: Mrs. Grossman's
Idea to note: Andy downloaded several blueprints for skateboard ramps from the Internet and used them as background paper.

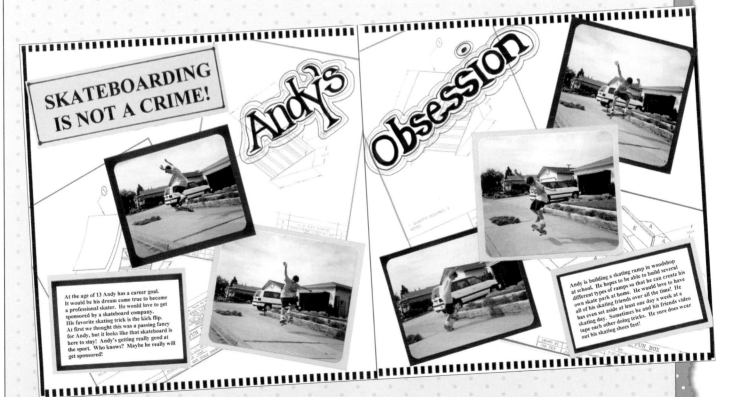

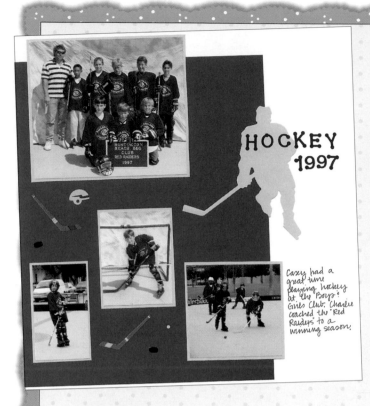

HOCKEY
1997

Caxey had a great time playing hockey at "the Boys & Girls Club." Charlie coached the "Red Raiders" to a winning season.

PETER SKATING IN BACK YARD- JANUARY, 1997   MITCH SHOWING THE ROPES!   "OUCH!"

"Hockey Kid"
by Deb Day
Coon Rapids, Minnesota
SUPPLIES
Die cuts: Accu-Cut Systems;
Punky Doodle
Pens: LePlume, Marvy Uchida
Star stamps: Stamps by Judith
Scissors: Victorian edge, Fiskars

"Hockey 1997"
by Colleen Adams
Huntington Beach, California
SUPPLIES
Stickers: Mrs. Grossman's
Letter stickers: Sticklers
Die cut: Accu-Cut Systems
Pen: Micron Pigma, Sakura

"Anoka Blues"
by Deb Day
Coon Rapids, Minnesota
SUPPLIES
Letter stickers: Creative Memories
Pens: LePlume, Marvy Uchida
Idea to note: Deb re-created the
team's emblem using markers.

ANOKA BLUES

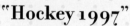

MITCH

96·97

ANOKA CLASSIC IN HOUS

THIS PHOTO APPEAR IN THE ANOKA UNION PAPER AFTER WINNING THE TOURNAMENT.

"CELEBRATE! CELEBRATE!"

FOGERTY ICE ARENA - BLAINE

SAM TOOK SKATING LESSONS WITH TRACY DEROSIER - FEB. 1997

"Skating Lessons"

by Deb Day
Coon Rapids, Minnesota

SUPPLIES

Star stamp: Stamps by Judith
Die cuts: Ellison
Stickers: Creative Memories
Pen: Micron Pigma, Sakura
Large star template: Provo Craft

"Gymnastics"

by Kerri Bradford
Orem, Utah

SUPPLIES

Stickers: Mrs. Grossman's
Scissors: Deckle edge, Fiskars

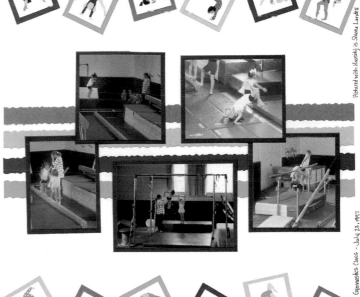

Pictured with Kristin is Shani Luttrell

Gymnastics Class - July 23, 1997

4 Wheelin'

"Four Wheelin'"

by Lynette Staker
Provo, Utah

SUPPLIES

Die cut: All My Memories
Scissors: Peaks and Stamp edges, Fiskars
Pen: Zig Opaque Writer, EK Success
Idea to note: To give the tire wheels extra "traction,"
Lynette cropped them with the Stamp-edge scissors.

"Gone Fishing"

by Megan Staker
Provo, Utah
SUPPLIES
Stickers: The Gifted Line
Pen: Zig Opaque Writer, EK Success
Corner edger: Victorian edge, Fiskars

"Sportsman's Paradise"

by Janie Thomas
Blakely, Georgia
SUPPLIES
Paper: Creative Memories
Letter stickers: Creative Memories
Stickers: Creative Memories
Ruler: Borderlines, Creative Memories
Pen: Micron Pigma, Sakura
Scissors: Deckle edge, Fiskars

Johnathan, Matt and Kelly are

REELING 'EM IN

at **CAMP EVERS!**

May, 1998

"Reeling 'Em In"

by Dianne Gottron
Memories
San Jose, California

SUPPLIES

Letter stickers: Making Memories
Circle cutter: Making Memories
Stickers: Mrs. Grossman's; Frances Meyer
Pens: Studio 2; Zig Ball, EK Success
Laminate: Xyron
Idea to note: How did Dianne create this net full of fish? She simply laminated the stickers using Xyron's double-sided lamination cartridge.

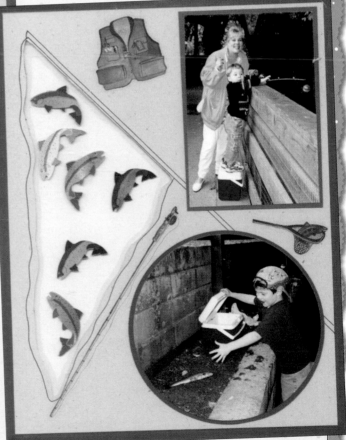

We all had a great time! We couldn't get 'em off the hooks fast enough...

Those trout were wriggly, squiggly, fun and YUMMY!

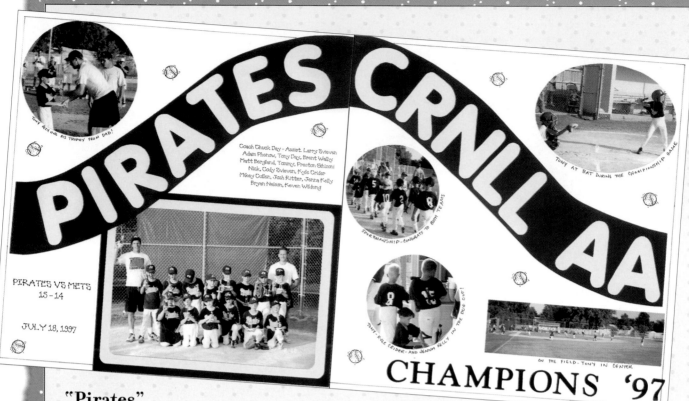

PIRATES CRNLL AA

Coach Chuck Day - Assist. Larry Svieven
Adam Phanow, Tony Day, Brent Walby
Matt Berglund, Tommy, Preston Echizeni
Nick, Cody Svieven, Kyle Crider
Mikey Culler, Josh Ritter, Jenna Kelly
Bryan Nelson, Keven Wildung

TONY RECEIVING HIS TROPHY FROM DAD!

TONY AT BAT DURING THE CHAMPIONSHIP GAME

SPORTMANSHIP - CONGRATS TO BOTH TEAMS

PIRATES VS METS
15 - 14

JULY 18, 1997

TONY-KYLE CRIDER- AND JENNA KELLY IN THE DUG OUT!

ON THE FIELD. TONY IN CENTER

CHAMPIONS '97

"Pirates"

by Deb Day
Coon Rapids, Minnesota

SUPPLIES

Letter stickers: Creative Memories
Two-inch letter stencils: Trend
Templates: Creative Memories
Baseball stamp: D.J. Inkers

"Little League"

by Colleen Adams
Huntington Beach, California

SUPPLIES

Die cuts: Ellison
Stickers: Frances Meyer
Letter stickers: Sticklers
Baseball paper: Paper Pizazz,
Hot Off The Press
Pens: Micron Pigma, Sakura

LITTLE LEAGUE

Coach Pitch
Red Sox
1996

Casey and Coach Denny Chapman

After a slow start Casey really enjoyed his first season in Coach Pitch. At the end of the year his coach, Denny Chapman said that at first he thought Casey was just in Little League for the uniform, but that he turned out to be the heart of the team. We were very proud.

Ali Wilson cheering for the T-wolves.

Tricia Dockendorf's Tim Read

GO TEAM!

A few of us devoted Timberwolf fans drove up to Alta for the game. We lost 69 to 0, so as it may seem, we had to amuse ourselves!

FRIDAY, SEPTEMBER 19, 1997

"THS @ Alta"

by Jessica Stevenson
Orem, Utah

SUPPLIES

Paper: ScrapEase, What's New
Scissors: Deckle edge, Fiskars
Pens: Zig Clean Color, EK Success; Gelly Roll, Sakura
Paw-print stamp: Rubber Stamp Emporium

March 21, 1998

HUNTER EDUCATION GRADUATE
MONTANA
FISH, WILDLIFE & PARKS

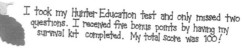

I took my Hunter Education test and only missed two questions. I received five bonus points by having my survival kit completed. My total score was 100!

"Hunter Education"

by Angie Peterson
Absarokee, Montana

SUPPLIES

Birch leaf punch: Family Treasures
Circle cutter: Creative Memories
Letter stickers: Creative Memories
Pen: Micron Pigma, Sakura

May 1995

TENNIS

"What a challenge! Jeremy pulled out our entire season in the tiebreaker. He did something we'll talk about for years." *Mt. Airy News,* May 17, 1995

"Tennis"

by Joyce Schweitzer
Greensboro, North Carolina

SUPPLIES

Die cut: Ellison
Stickers: Mrs. Grossman's
Scissors: Ripple edge, Fiskars
Pens: Micron Pigma, Sakura
Tennis racket and court: Joyce's own design
Idea to note: Joyce included a quote from the newspaper.

the Franklin Quest Championship at Park Meadows, Park City, UT

Lee Trevino

Park Meadows was just one of the stops on the PGA tour. I gave Sean tickets for Father's Day. He and Mark Hale went together.

AUG. 1996

Arnold Palmer

Arnold waiting his turn...and watching...

Dave Stockton Ready to Play.

Arnold Palmer, Lee Trevino and Dave Stockton were just three of the favorites on the tour.

Aug. 1996

"Golfing Championship"
by Sandi Lyman
Salem, Oregon
SUPPLIES
Stamps: D.O.T.S.
Paper: Close to my Heart; The Paper Patch
Pens: Tombow
Die cuts: Pebbles in my Pocket
Stationery: ScrapEase, What's New
Scissors: Pinking, Wave, Dragonback and Deckle edges, Fiskars

"Golfing with Dad"
by Cindy Lindborg
Niles, Michigan
SUPPLIES
Die cuts: Ellison
Scissors: Mini-Pinking and Leaf edges, Fiskars
Punches: Family Treasures; Marvy Uchida
Letter stamps: Hero Arts; Inkadinkadoo
Templates: Creative Memories;
C-Thru Ruler Co.

Paper: Paperbilities, MPR; The Paper Patch
Idea to note: Cindy ran the golf-ball paper through the Xyron adhesive system, and then stamped letters on the golf balls. Then, she centered the circle punch over each golf ball and punched them out—leaving her with perfect golf balls. Next, she just peeled the backing and stuck the balls on her page.

"River Rafting"

by Amber McDonald
Las Vegas, Nevada

SUPPLIES

Paper: Paper Pizazz, Hot Off The Press
Scissors: Pinking edge, Fiskars
Stickers: Provo Craft
Pens: Zig Memory System, EK Success
Idea to note: Highlight main points in your journaling with coordinating colors.

"Adventures in Duck Watchin'"

by Kaelene Bailey
Mesa, Arizona

SUPPLIES

Stickers: Mrs. Grossman's
Pen: Micron Pigma, Sakura
Lettering: Kaelene got the idea for this lettering from the "Indiana Jones" series of movies.

"Snow Trip"
by Elaine Schwertner
Lubbock, Texas
SUPPLIES
Computer font: Snowdrift,
Microsoft Word
Pens: Gelly Roll, Sakura
Trees: Elaine's own design
Paper: Close to my Heart

"Ski Utah"
by Vicki Garner
Memories By Design
Layton, Utah
SUPPLIES
Stickers: Stickopotamus
Pen: Zig Writer, EK Success

"3-on-3 Soccer"

by Lynette Staker
Provo, Utah

SUPPLIES

Scissors: Deckle edge, Family Treasures
Die cut: Ellison
Pens: Zig Writer and Zig Opaque Writer,
EK Success
Paper: The Paper Patch
Banner template: Provo Craft

"YMCA Soccer"

by Mary Lee Burton
Roosevelt, Utah

SUPPLIES

Paper: Paper Pizazz, Hot Off The Press
Scissors: Stamp edge, Fiskars
Stickers: Paper Magic
Idea to note: Mary Lee wanted to preserve
her son's awards and certificates, so she
color-copied them and included the copies
in her scrapbook.

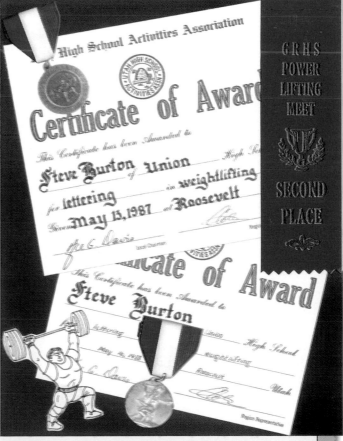

"Catch of the Day"

by Terry Larkin
Flint, Michigan

SUPPLIES

Stickers: Creative Memories;
Mrs. Grossman's
Fish die cuts: Ellison
Template: Creative Memories
Seaweed: Terry's own design

"The Lake"

by Dave Larkin
Flint, Michigan

SUPPLIES

Ruler: Borderlines, Creative Memories
Idea to note: Create letters from your photos.

"Kurt's Birthday"

by Megan Fowler
Memories By Design
Layton, Utah

SUPPLIES

Stickers: Stickopotamus; Mrs. Grossman's
Letter stickers: Frances Meyer
Idea to note: Megan color-copied and enlarged her
stickers to add a fun embellishment.

"Lake Powell"

by Lynette Staker
Provo, Utah

SUPPLIES

Pen: Zig Opaque Writer and Zig Writer, EK Success
Lettering template: Frances Meyer
Stickers: Mrs. Grossman's

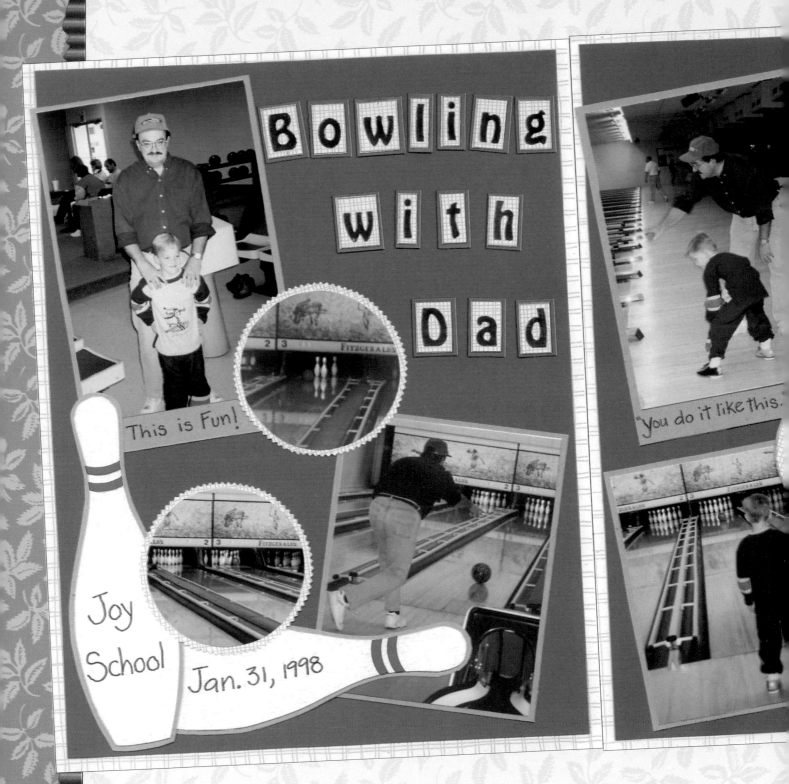

Bowling with Dad

This is Fun!

Joy School   Jan. 31, 1998

"You do it like this.

FAMILY TIMES

When times get hard and you

need a shoulder to lean on,

you can always count on your family.

They're there to support you,

laugh with you, and sometimes

even cry with you. You'll find some

fabulous ways to showcase your

family ties with the creative

examples found in this section.

"Bowling with Dad"
by Cherylanne Strong
Roy, Utah
SUPPLIES
Scissors: Mini-Pinking edge, Fiskars
Die cuts: Ellison
Paper: Northern Spy
Font: Hobby Headline, Print Artist
Pen: Zig Writer, EK Success

Scissors: Spindle edge by Fiskars; Border paper: Hot Off the Press.

"A Time to Plant"

by Susan Gilmore
Oviedo, Florida

SUPPLIES
Stickers: Mrs. Grossman's
Letter stickers: Creative Memories
Pen: Micron Pigma, Sakura

"What a Day"

by Elizabeth Weeks
Yuma, Arizona

SUPPLIES
Craft punches: Family Treasures
Scissors: Deckle edge, Fiskars
Large sun: Elizabeth's own design
Pen: Micron Pigma, Sakura; Hybrid Roller (gold), Pentel

A TIME TO PLANT

And a time to uproot

There is a time for everything and a season for every activity under heaven.

Ecclesiastes ch. 3

Connor and PePop plant some vegetables

April '98

What do we do on a Saturday? March 21, 1998

We start the day out at the gym, and today Evy had a haircut. Back home we play ~ Zac likes his cave in the blanket. Dad had to work so we brought him lunch.

What a Day!

and grabbed an ice cream snack! Evy gets a little work done on her scrapbooks and bar-b-ques chicken in the smoker ~ Zac's favorite with rice!

November 1986

WE LOVE FALL

Armco Park

"We Love Fall"

by Joyce Schweitzer
Greensboro, North Carolina

SUPPLIES

Scissors: Ripple, Zipper and Jigsaw edges, Fiskars
Pen: Micron Pigma, Sakura
Paper: Paper Pizazz, Hot Off The Press
Letter template: Pebble Tracers, Pebbles in my Pocket
Maple leaf punch: Family Treasures

"Comics"

by Joyce Schweitzer
Greensboro, North Carolina

SUPPLIES

Pens: Micron Pigma, Sakura
Stickers: Creative Memories
Idea to note: Joyce traced comic strips right from a newspaper and then colored them in with pens.

THE FAMILY CIRCUS

HA! FOOLED YOU, DIDN'T I? TOO QUICK FOR YOU, WASN'T I?

COMICS

Every time that I'm your herder
You think you get away with murder.
All right, Brandon, so you do;
But only because I want you to!

SNUFFY SMITH

TH' ONLY TIME THAT WILD YOUNG-UN AIN'T TEARIN' UP SOMETHING— --IS WHEN HE'S SOUND ASLEEP

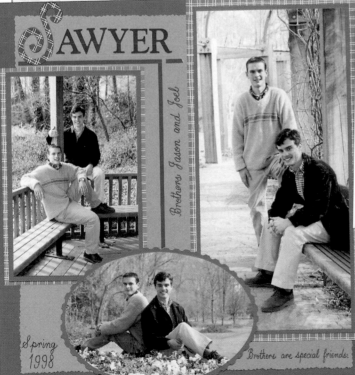

SAWYER

Brothers Jason and Joel

Spring 1998

Brothers are special friends.

"Sawyer Brothers"

by Joyce Schweitzer
Greensboro, North Carolina

SUPPLIES

Paper: Northern Spy
Stickers: Mrs. Grossman's
Letter stickers: Creative Memories
Scissors: Deckle and Jigsaw edges, Fiskars
Letter template: Pebble Tracers, Pebbles in my Pocket

"Woodruff Daily News"

by Tonya Woodruff
Tremonton, Utah

SUPPLIES

Scissors: Deckle edge, Fiskars
Computer font: Futura Medium Condensed, Print Artist
Idea to note: Use your home computer to create your own "Family Times."

WOODRUFF DAILY NEWS

MARCH 21, 1998   TREMONTON, UT   VOL. XOXO

"WOODRUFF FAMILY TRAVELS TO DISNEY'S TOY STORY ON ICE"

SALT LAKE CITY OR BUST!

Feature article written by: Nate & Kelsey's Mom

Thanks to Uncle Jeff, we found out that it was time to buy tickets to Disney on Ice. We really wanted to go this year because it was "Toy Story".

When Mom picked us up after she got off work on January 27, 1998, we ordered our tickets. They were on Row 8 right next to the bleacher's seats. Now comes the hard part! — the waiting. March 21st seems soooo far away!!

The day FINALLY came. Kelsey had had a friend spend the night & they had stayed up really late. Mom had to be up early to make cinnamon rolls for a Relief Society party. Nate had some writing/playing to take care of. And Dad had to go finish a writing job before we could leave.

To the kids it seemed like forever before we were ready to leave for Salt Lake City. The kids were so excited that Mom and Dad just knew that it would be a noisy 1 1/2 hour drive with 2 very enthusiastic children. But to the surprise of everyone — Kelsey & Nate fell asleep. And Mom & Dad enjoyed a very quite drive. What a treat!

(Story cont. on page W2)

WOODRUFF DAILY NEWS

MARCH 21, 1998   TREMONTON, UT   PAGE W2

(Cont. from Front Page)

Just a few of our favorite things about "Toy Story":

Dad: The green army men!

Mom: The "claw" & the toys in Sid's room!

Kelsey: At the end when Mr. Potato Head finds out that their is a Mrs. Potato Head and he says, "I've got to shave", and he pulls off his mustache and throws it & at the end when there's a new dinosaur for T-Rex & when he sees her she has wings & turns real mean & growls at him!

Nate: Buzz & Woody!

The program was held in the "Delta Center". We arrived in plenty of time to get goodies and prizes. We like to buy slushies & cotton candy when we come. Nate also got a Buzz Lightyear sword & Kelsey got a Disney coloring book.

It was the best show ever!!! We had a great time and can hardly wait until it's time to come again next year.

(See page W3 for Photo Feature)

WOODRUFF DAILY NEWS

MARCH 21, 1998   TREMONTON, UT   PAGE W3

TOY STORY PHOTO FEATURE

"Burger King Celebration"

by Diana Pishion
The Dalles, Oregon

SUPPLIES

Circle cutter: Creative Memories
Scissors: Deckle and Ripple edges, Fiskars
Pen: Micron Pigma, Sakura

"The 'Starrs' Are Out Tonight"

by Gretchen Starr
McPherson, Kansas

SUPPLIES

Die cuts: Ellison
Stickers: Stickopotamus; Creative Memories
Pen: Zig Writer, EK Success

"Byron's Family"

by Marsha Peacock
Jacksonville, Florida

SUPPLIES

Pens: LePlume, Marvy Uchida; Zig Opaque Writer,
EK Success; Micron Pigma, Sakura
Template: Border Buddy, EK Success
Scissors: Scallop edge, Fiskars
Stickers: Mrs. Grossman's
Die-cut house: Ellison
Idea to note: Marsha used a ruler and an Opaque
Writer to create "bricks," the Border Buddy
and a black pen to create the "shingles," and Scallop-
edged scissors for "smoke."

"Parade of Homes"

by Sharon Erickson
Camarillo, California

SUPPLIES

Paper: The Paper Patch
Stickers: Mrs. Grossman's; Creative Memories
Scissors: Scallop, Clouds, Colonial and Peaks edges,
Fiskars
Heart punch: McGill
Pens: Micron Pigma, Sakura
Idea to note: Create your own "parade of homes"
by highlighting homes you've lived in, how long you lived
there, and how much they cost.

Hearts Knit Together... With Love.

April 7, 1996

"Laundry"
by Deanna Furey
Jacksonville, Florida
SUPPLIES
Stickers: Mrs. Grossman's
Paper: The Paper Patch
Scissors: Jumbo Deckle edge, Family Treasures
Rubber stamp: Art Impressions
Laundry clip art: Source unknown

"Knitting"
by Denise Wood
Lakewood, Colorado
SUPPLIES
Scissors: Colonial edge, Fiskars
Templates: Provo Craft
Pen: Zig Millennium, EK Success;
LePlume II, Marvy Uchida
Knitting needles and yarn: Denise's own design

an ordinary day in my life!

Saturday, March 21, 1998
Sleep in until 8:00 a.m.! Feed the family breakfast, and then head to Si View Park to meet the Cub Scouts.

Bens room before

Scouting for food - bag distribution day. The rain started when we started. The cubs present are Neil Lequia, Josh and Alex Hart, Keith Keller, Jake Tweten and Ben Garding.

Mom starts the drilling to put up the shelves in Ben's room.

and after

Well, it took four hours but the room looks great!

"An Ordinary Day"

by Diane Garding
North Bend, Washington

SUPPLIES

Paper: The Paper Patch
Craft punches: Family Treasures
Stickers: Suzy's Zoo
Stationery: Sonburn
Pens: Micron Pigma, Sakura

November 8, 1997

Eric Snodgrass & Tracy Clements

Gabby & Uncle Eric

"Denim and Daisies"

by Nikki Probert
Belton, Missouri

SUPPLIES

Pen: Callipen, Sakura
Die cut: Accu-Cut Systems
Paper: Paperbilities, MPR

"Denim Days"

by Kelly Robinson
Campbell, California

SUPPLIES

Paper: Close to my Heart
Letter template: D.O.T.S.
Flower punch: Family Treasures
Pen: Scrapbook Writer,
Close to my Heart
Scissors: Deckle edge, Fiskars

Misty & Faith

Joshua & Kelly Robinson

Joshua 3 years old

March 1998

A flower for Mom

In a field of flowers we found

DENIM DAYS

"Just Hanging Around"

by Jennae Snow
St. George, Utah

SUPPLIES

Letter template: Pebble Tracers, Pebbles in my Pocket
Stickers: Stickopotamus
Hole punches: Punch Line, McGill
Palm-tree stencil: Cherished Memories
Die cuts: Ellison; Pebbles in my Pocket

"Family Reunion"

by Jessica Stevenson
Orem, Utah

SUPPLIES

Paper: Provo Craft
Pens: Zig Writer and Zig Opaque
Writer, EK Success
Idea to note: Jessica cut the fence,
bunny and grass out of a piece of
Provo Craft stationery, then
adhered them to another piece of
Provo Craft paper.

It was delightful watching the kids dig themselves deep in the sand. - They were so cute - packing the sand tightly around their sweet feet and then fighting to break free of their grainy prison. Pictures were taken Memorial Day, 1998 at the Orem, Utah Park.

Jacob, Ashley, Aimee and Emily - May, 1998

the White kids

The Staker family

JUNE 1998

"The White Kids"

by Shauna White
Idaho Falls, Idaho

SUPPLIES

Pen: Zig Writer, EK Success
Colored pencils: Prisma Color, Berol
Idea to note: Shauna tore two different shades of paper to make a pile of sand. She then silhouetted her photo and tucked it into the "sand."

"The Staker Family"

by Sara Staker
Provo, Utah

SUPPLIES

Paper: Over The Moon Press
Stickers: Mrs. Grossman's
Pen: Zig Opaque Writer, EK Success
Punches: Family Treasures
Photo corners: Line Co.

Halloween

JennyLee ~ 4 years Old ~ 1991

~5 Years Later~

JennyLee ~

~1996~

Jenny loves to

SEASONAL SNAPSHOTS

Celebrate each holiday throughout the

year with these festive page examples.

Whether you're hunting for pastel-colored

Easter eggs or "oohing" and "ahhing"

over the colorful bursts of fireworks

on the Fourth, you're sure to find

plenty of inspiration here. So pull out

those pictures of ghosts and goblins,

and scare yourself up some

spooky scrapbook pages.

"Halloween"

by LeAnn Palmer
South Jordan, Utah

SUPPLIES

Scissors: Deckle and Bubbles edges,
Fiskars
Die cuts: Ellison (cauldron, flowers,
bat, spider); Accu-Cut Systems (fire,
bones)
Circle punches: Family Treasures
Hole punch: Punch Line, McGill
Pens: Zig Writer, EK Success

Scissors: Clouds edge by Fiskars.

"Making Valentines"

by Cherylanne Strong
Roy, Utah

SUPPLIES

Paper: Northern Spy
Heart punch: Family Treasures
Pens: Micron Pigma, Sakura
Computer font: Mead Bold, Print Artist
Photo corners: Canson
Heart: Cherylanne's own design
Star Wars pictures: Cut from valentine cards
Idea to note: Cherylanne color-copied her son's valentine to include on her layout and made a pocket page to hold his valentines.

"Love"

by Patty Clark
Grayslake, Illinois

SUPPLIES

Pens: Zig Writer, EK Success
Scissors: Scallop edge, Fiskars
Stickers: Mrs. Grossman's
Heart: Patty's own design

February 1997

Roses is red
Violets be blue
Gi Gi are sweet!
We love you!
Ain't that phat!

My original poetry and homemade Valentine to Gigi... Plus an anonymous humongous Valentine balloon make another fun album page!

"Roses Are Red"

by Joyce Schweitzer
Greensboro, North Carolina

SUPPLIES

Scissors: Ripple, Scallop and Seagull (corner) edges, Fiskars
Stickers: Mrs. Grossman's
Pen: Micron Pigma, Sakura

"Lucky Day"

by Shana Blackham
Englewood, Colorado

SUPPLIES

Die cuts: Ellison
Shamrock template: Source unknown
Paper: The Paper Patch
Stickers: Mrs. Grossman's; Stickopotamus
Pen: Zig Calligraphy, EK Success

March 18, 1997

Lucky Us We have YOU!

"Yum! This chocolate is so good!"

Look at what we found!

Easter April 1996 Albuquerque, N.M.

"Josh, there's an egg right here!"

★ Mom and Dad hid eggs for our Easter Egg Hunt. ★

"C'mon, Josh, I see some eggs!"

"Easter Egg Hunt"

by Kim Melanson
Albuquerque, New Mexico

SUPPLIES

Die cuts: Ellison
Pen: Zig Millennium, EK Success
Scissors: Pinking edge, Fiskars

"Easter 1997"

by Tamberly Case
Flint, Michigan

SUPPLIES

Letter stickers: Creative Memories
Stickers: Mrs. Grossman's
Stamp pads: ColorBox, Clearsnap, Inc.
Pens: Micron Pigma, Sakura
Scissors: Deckle edge, Fiskars
Idea to note: Tamberly used make-up sponges to create the powdery, pastel background.

"T. J.'s First Easter"

by Gayle Holdman
American Fork, Utah

SUPPLIES

Paper: Gayle created her own plaid design using Tombow markers.
Die cuts: Ellison
Pens: Tombow
Stamps: Stampin' Up!; D.O.T.S
Stamp pads: Marvy Uchida

It was raining, I hunted for my Easter basket inside. It was a Peter Pan Easter basket. I dyed Easter eggs with Grandpa Bix. We colored the eggs.

EASTER FUN

1998

"Finders, Keepers"

by Marlene Bixenman
Ontario, California
SUPPLIES
Paper: Creative Memories
Letter stickers: Frances Meyer (white); Creative Memories (blue)
Stickers: Mrs. Grossman's
Templates: Puzzle Mates, Quick Cuts
Pens: Micron Pigma, Sakura

"Mother's Day"

by Jewelene Holverson
Pocatello, Idaho
SUPPLIES
Stamp pads: ColorBox, Clearsnap, Inc.
Pens: Micron Pigma, Sakura, LePlume, Marvy Uchida
Scissors: Stamp edge, Fiskars
Idea to note: There's no longer any need to worry about messy fingerprints. Jewelene used her ten digits to create this wonderful garden scene.

All five of us kids created and compiled a scrapbook for mom on Mother's Day. She was thrilled over her surprise... even to tears. She enjoyed reminiscing through each page.

"I Love Daddy"

by Debra Wilcox
Karen Foster Design
Farmington, Utah

SUPPLIES

Paper: Karen Foster Design; Close to my Heart; Hot Off The Press

Die cuts: Ellison

Letter template: Pebble Tracers, Pebbles in my Pocket

Scissors: Scallop, Mini-Pinking and Seagull edges, Fiskars

"This Land Is My Land"

by Kim Cook
The Heartland Paper Co.
Bountiful, Utah

SUPPLIES

Paper: Provo Craft; The Paper Patch; Main Street Press, Ltd.

Sticky die cuts: Provo Craft

Craft punches: Marvy Uchida; Punch Line, McGill

Pens: Zig Opaque Writer, EK Success

"Red, White and Blue"

by LeAnn Palmer
South Jordan, Utah

SUPPLIES

Die cuts: Ellison
Star punches: McGill; Family Treasures
Scissors: Deckle edge, Fiskars
Pens: Gelly Roll, Sakura

"Fourth of July Weekend"

by Tawni Walton
Loomis, Nebraska

SUPPLIES

Stickers: Mrs. Grossman's
Pens: Micron Pigma, Sakura; Pentel
Flag and stars: Tawni's own design

"A Pirate's Life for Me"

by Teryl Zollinger
Declo, Idaho

SUPPLIES

Scissors: Wave edge, Fiskars
Computer font: Beguiat and Technical, WordPerfect
Boat: Teryl's own design
Idea to note: Teryl used a circle template to create the waves.

A Pirate's Life is the Life for Me !

AHOY MATEY!
It's Halloween 1996...
Clayne Stirland and his brother, Kyle, both decided to dress up as pirates this year. Mom made all the costumes, including the hats, which was no easy task. Clayne was all decked out with a bandana, hat, eye patch and an earring! Boy, did that hurt!
Even though they enjoyed dressing up, the best part of the evening was the CANDY!

I'm bringing home a BABY BUMBLEBEE won't my mommy be so proud of me!

Happy Halloween!

"Happy Halloween"

by Laura Thompson
Spanish Fork, Utah

SUPPLIES

Stickers: Mrs. Grossman's; Suzy's Zoo
Die cut: Ellison
Pen: Micron Pigma, Sakura

"Creepy"

by Regan Bryan
Stansbury Park, Utah

SUPPLIES

Paper: The Paper Patch
Circle template: Provo Craft
Pen: Zig Clean Color, EK Success
Spiders' legs: Regan's own design
Idea to note: Regan added legs to the exclamation point to create a spider.

CREEPY!

Jeremy (7), Regan (5), Sarah (3), and Jeanna Gardner (6)

Halloween 1985

"Then and Now"

by Melissa Sandoval
Cerritos, California

SUPPLIES

Die cuts: Ellison
Stickers: Stickopotamus
Paper: The Paper Patch
Letter stamps: Source unknown
Stamp pads: ColorBox, Clearsnap, Inc.

"Trick or Treat"

Breneé Williams
Boise, Idaho

SUPPLIES

Paper: Close to my Heart
Stamp: D.O.T.S.
Stamp pad: Marvy Uchida
Pens: Micron Pigma, Sakura;
Zig Writer, FK Success
Pumpkins: Breneé's own design

"How to Carve a Pumpkin"

by Chiara Willis
Bowling Green, Ohio

SUPPLIES

Pens: Zig Writer, EK Success
Stickers: Stickopotamus
Idea to note: Using a circle cutter, Chiara created her own "pumpkins" to show the progression of the jack-o-lantern.

"Just Us Girls"

by Lindsey Smith
Orem, Utah

SUPPLIES

Paper: The Paper Patch; Paper Adventures
Letter stickers: Pebbles in my Pocket
Pen: Gelly Roll, Sakura

"Halloween 1997"

by Marci Leishman
Draper, Utah

SUPPLIES

Letter stickers: Frances Meyer
Stickers: Provo Craft
Pen: Zig Writer, EK Success

"Let Us Give Thanks"

by Joyce Schweitzer
Greensboro, North Carolina

SUPPLIES

Paper: Paperbilities, MPR; The Paper Patch
Turkey die cut: Source unknown
Letter template: Pebble Tracers, Pebbles in my Pocket
Scissors: Ripple and Seagull (corner) edges, Fiskars
Pens: Micron Pigma, Sakura; Zig Opaque Writer, EK Success
Punches: Family Treasures; McGill; Marvy Uchida
Scarecrow pattern: "Scrapbooks for Painters" (Joyce traced the scarecrow, cut it out and then assembled it.)
Idea to note: To make your own crow, create the body with the large heart punch, use the birch leaf punch to create wings, the medium circle punch to create the head, the small star to create the beak, the small snowflake punch for the feet, and the micro punch to create the crows' eyes.

"Pilgrim's Hat"

by Sheila Smith
Tupelo, Mississippi

SUPPLIES

Pens: Callipen and Micron Pigma, Sakura
Stickers: Mrs. Grossman's
Die cuts: Creative Memories
Idea to note: Sheila re-created the pilgrim's hat pictured in her photo.

"Thanksgiving"

by Angelyn Bryce
West Chester, Pennsylvania

SUPPLIES

Maple leaf punch: Marvy Uchida
Scissors: Clouds edge, Fiskars
Cornucopia and vine: Angelyn's own design

"Fall Fun"

by Laura Thompson
Spanish Fork, Utah

SUPPLIES

Paper: Keeping Memories Alive
Stickers: Mrs. Grossman's; Provo Craft
Pen: Micron Pigma, Sakura
Idea to note: Laura included a souvenir she picked up on her outing.

"Hanukkah"

by Robin Camhi
West Hills, California

SUPPLIES

Die cuts: Creative Memories
Paper: Frances Meyer
Pen: Micron Pigma, Sakura
Letter stickers: Creative Memories
Scissors: Deckle edge, Fiskars

BON VOYAGE

The suitcases are packed,

the tickets are tucked safely in

your purse, and you're ready for

a week of relaxation. Whether you've

got a secluded vacation retreat or

you're heading to the bustle of

Disneyland, you're in for a real

adventure with these fresh

vacation pages.

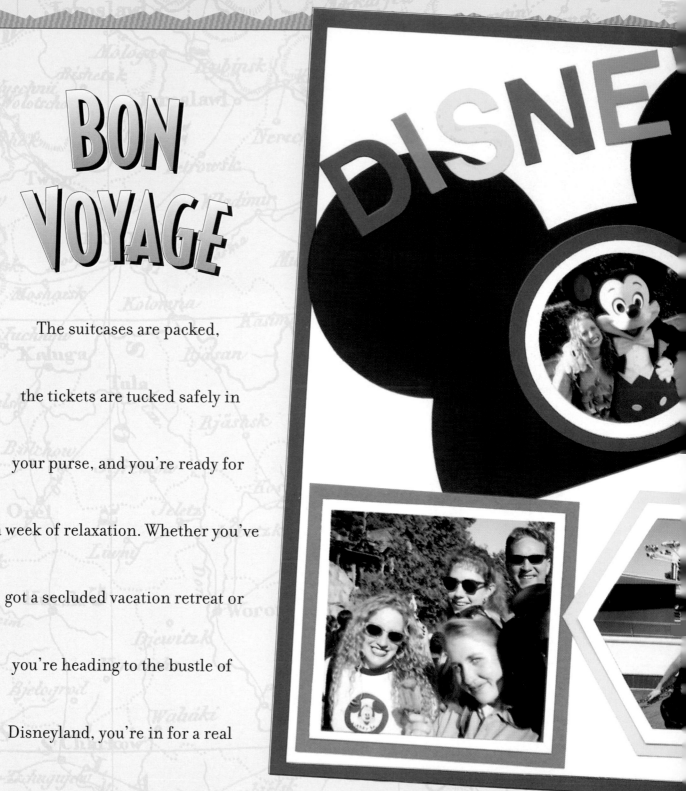

"Disneyland"
Karen Petersen
Mom and Me Scrapbooking
Salt Lake City, Utah
SUPPLIES
Letter die cuts: Ellison
Mickey Mouse ears and Donald Duck hat: Karen's
own design

Scissors: Bow tie edge by Fiskars.

LAND

TROPICALE
1996

"Tropicale 1996"

by Jan Northington
Los Osos, California

SUPPLIES

Pens: Callipen and Micron Pigma, Sakura
Scissors: Clouds and Scallop edges, Fiskars
Ruler: Borderlines, Creative Memories
Stickers: Stickopotamus
Letter stickers: Creative Memories

"Las Vegas"

by Sharon Erickson
Camarillo, California

SUPPLIES

Corner edger: Art Deco, Fiskars
Large star stickers: Frances Meyer
Stickers: Mrs. Grossman's
Letter stickers: Creative Memories
Craft punches: McGill
Pens: Callipen and Micron Pigma, Sakura

"Under the Arbor"

by Carole Kamradt
The Paper Attic
Sandy, Utah

SUPPLIES

Maple leaf punch: Family Treasures
Hole punch (⅛"): Punch Line, McGill
Pen: Gelly Roll, Sakura
Other: Branches and arbor are Carole's own design.
Idea to note: Carole used the ⅛" hole punch to create bunches of grapes.

"Boothill Graveyard"

by Sharon Lewis
Memory Lane
Mesa, Arizona

SUPPLIES

Blitzer: Inkworx
Pens: Micron Pigma and Pen Touch Paint
Marker, Sakura
Star punch: Marvy Uchida
Scissors: Deckle and Leaf edges, Fiskars
Wood paper: Frances Meyer
Idea to note: Sharon created the cactus with
Fiskars' Leaf-edge scissors.

In October we took melanie to Disney World for the first time. At first she didn't know what to think in the magic kingdom. After a few rides in fantasy land she was prancing and dancing all over the place! It was a magical vacation and melanie the perfect age - almost 4 years old.

"Disney World"

by Marsha Peacock
Jacksonville, Florida

SUPPLIES

Paper: Paper Pizazz, Hot Off The Press
Scissors: Clouds edge, Fiskars
Pens: LePlume, Marvy Uchida
Cloud stencil: Printworks Design
Idea to note: Marsha sponged around a cloud stencil with pens to create the background.

"Sea World"

by Sandy Zwicker
Timeless Treasures
Santa Margarita, California

SUPPLIES

Die cuts: Accu-Cut Systems
Pen: Zig Writer, EK Success

Winnie
the
Pooh
and
Tigger
too

October 15, 1997

Pluto

minnie mouse

"Disneyland"

by Deanna Holdsworth
Alta Loma, California

SUPPLIES

Paper: Paper Pizazz, Hot Off The Press
Letter template: Pebble Tracers,
Pebbles in my Pocket
Pen: Zig Writer, EK Success

Teacup ride
and
Toontown

flying
Dumbo
ride

carousel

toontown rollercoaster

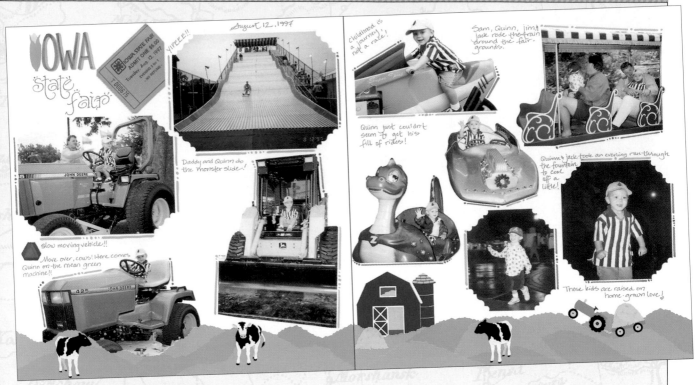

"Iowa State Fair"

by Amy Carrell
Des Moines, Iowa

SUPPLIES

Scissors: Deckle and Majestic edges, Fiskars
Stickers: Mrs. Grossman's
Pens: LePlume, Marvy Uchida
Idea to note: Amy used two shades of green to create rolling hills.

"A Day at the Fair"

by Beth Rogers
Mesa, Arizona

SUPPLIES

Letter stickers: Creative Memories
Stickers: Mrs. Grossman's
Cloud punch: Family Treasures

Die cuts: Ellison
Pens: Micron Pigma, Sakura
Stamp pad: D.O.T.S.
Hot dog: Beth's own design
Idea to note: Create your own cotton candy with a make-up sponge and a stamp pad.

MOAB
March 21, 1998

Our hike at Arches was awesome. A little rain, some wind, and a lot of hail didn't stop us. We hiked long and hard and it was well worth it. Delicate Arch was great. Later we biked at Slick Rock. What a super day.

"Moab"
by MarJean Boyter
Hooper, Utah
SUPPLIES
Southwest paper-piecing pattern: Windows of Time

ARIZONA

The day after Thanksgiving we decided to go hiking and work off that pumpkin pie. It turned out to be a beautiful day.

Mom and SueEllen hiking in Phoenix, AZ on November 26, 1997

"Arizona"
by Leah Marks
DogByte Development
Los Angeles, California
SUPPLIES
Computer program: DogByte Development
Scissors: Deckle edge, Fiskars
Cactus: Leah's own design

"Beach Time"

by Karen Petersen
Mom and Me Scrapbooking
Salt Lake City, Utah

SUPPLIES

Die cuts: Ellison
Craft punches: Family Treasures
Scissors: Ripple edge, Fiskars
Idea to note: Create a bumpy pile of sand with Fiskars' Ripple-edge scissors.

"San Francisco Maritime"

by Alaine Tanner
Maple Valley, Washington

SUPPLIES

Scissors: Clouds edge, Fiskars; Deckle edge, Family Treasures
Die cut: Accu-Cut Systems
Pen: Zig Writer, EK Success
Idea to note: Alaine used Fiskars' Clouds-edge scissors to create the rope.

"Puerto Vallarta, Mexico"

by Tanya Hancock
Portland, Oregon

SUPPLIES

Stickers: Mrs. Grossman's
Pen: Zig Writer, EK Success
Computer font idea: DJ Salsa, Dazzle Daze, D.J. Inkers
Mexico cutout: Tanya's own design

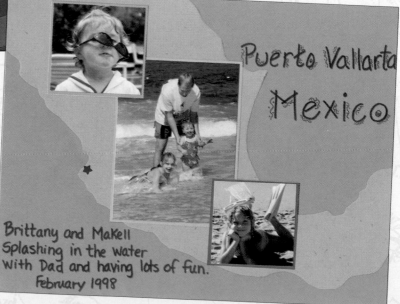

Brittany and Makell Splashing in the water with Dad and having lots of fun. February 1998

Puerto Vallarta Mexico

"Just Mauied"

by Molly Haskins
Rochester, Minnesota

SUPPLIES

Die cuts: ScrapEase, What's New
Stickers: Mrs. Grossman's
Paper: Paper Pizazz, Hot Off The Press
Ruler: Deja Views, C-Thru Ruler Co.
Pen: Zig Writer, EK Success

"Beach Fun"

by Sharon Erickson
Camarillo, California

SUPPLIES

Stickers: Frances Meyer; Mrs. Grossman's
Scissors: Colonial edge, Fiskars

"Florida"

by Debbie Meyer
Elida, Ohio

SUPPLIES

Letter die cuts: Creative Memories
Alligator die cut: Ellison
Star punch: Fiskars
Stickers: Mrs. Grossman's
Circle cutter: Creative Memories
Stamp pad: ColorBox, Clearsnap, Inc.
Florida cutout: Debbie's own design
Idea to note: Debbie made a large "orange" and cut out the center to create the perfect frame for her Polaroids.

"June 1997"

by Janie Thomas
Blakely, Georgia

SUPPLIES

Die cuts: Creative Memories
Pen: Micron Pigma, Sakura
Templates: C-Thru Ruler Co.; Creative Memories
Ruler: Borderlines, Creative Memories
Letter stickers: Making Memories

"Beach Baby"

by Breneé Williams
Boise, Idaho

SUPPLIES

Paper: Close to my Heart
"Fun in the Sun" paper: Source unknown
Scissors: Wave, Seagull and Ripple edges, Fiskars
Stickers: RA Lang; Mrs. Grossman's
Pen: Zig Writer, EK Success

"Myrtle Beach"

by Jana Lange
Raleigh, North Carolina

SUPPLIES

Stickers: Stickopotamus; Frances Meyer
Pens: LePlume II, Marvy Uchida
Boat and umbrella: Jana's own design

"Memorial Day Weekend"

by Angela Barrus
North Bend, Washington

SUPPLIES

Stickers: Provo Craft
Computer font: DJ Outline and DJ Desert, Fontastic!, D.J. Inkers
Scissors: Deckle edge, Fiskars

"Shoshone Falls"

by Kerri Bradford
Orem, Utah

SUPPLIES

Templates: Provo Craft
Stickers: Provo Craft

Letter stickers: Creative Memories
Scissors: Deckle edge, Fiskars
Waterfalls and hills: Kerri's own design
Idea to note: Kerri made the letters "fall" down the waterfall.

"Jackson Holc"

by Kirsten Wilson
Bountiful, Utah
SUPPLIES
Die cuts: Accu-Cut Systems

"Park City"

by Carole Kamradt
The Paper Attic
Sandy, Utah
SUPPLIES
Paper: Close to my Heart; Wubie;
Over the Moon Press
Template: Provo Craft

Rubber stamps: D.O.T.S.
Scissors: Deckle and Peaks edges,
Fiskars
Computer fonts: DJ Signpost,
Fontastic!, D.J. Inkers
Pens: Zig Millennium, EK Success; Pen
Touch Paint Marker, Sakura
Photo corners: Canson

"End of the Oregon Trail"

by Karen Preston
Portland, Oregon

SUPPLIES

Pen: Zig Calligraphy, EK Success
Covered wagon: Karen's own design

"Rainforest Café"

by Vangie Norton
Mesa, Arizona

SUPPLIES

Paper: The Paper Patch
Die cut: Ellison
Stickers: Melissa Neufeld, Inc.; Mrs. Grossman's
Flower punch: McGill
Pen: Zig Writer, EK Success
Idea to note: Vangie traced the "Rainforest Café" lettering from a napkin and cut the letters out.

March 21, 1998 ...
Outfitted in shorts, hats, and sunscreen, we headed to Bonniesprings Petting Zoo in beautiful Red Rock Canyon. What better way to spend the day!

Bonniesprings Petting Zoo

"Petting Zoo"

by Karri Payne
Las Vegas, Nevada

SUPPLIES

Paper: Northern Spy
Computer font: DJ Knobbish,
FiddleSticks, D.J. Inkers;
Marking Pen, Print Shop,
Broderbund

San Diego

ZOO

"San Diego Zoo"

by Sandy Zwicker
Timeless Treasures
Santa Margarita, California

SUPPLIES

Die cuts: Accu-Cut Systems
Scissors: Imperial edge, Fiskars
Craft punches: Family Treasures
Idea to note: Create your own lion by using the center of Accu-Cut Systems' sun die cut, and Family Treasures' large flower, small circle, small egg and heart border punches. To make the giraffe, simply use Family Treasures' large circle, small egg and mini heart punches.

"Lake Powell Trip"
by Karen Petersen
Mom and Me Scrapbooking
Salt Lake City, Utah

SUPPLIES
Die cut: Ellison
Stickers: Mrs. Grossman's
Computer font: Scrap Fiesta, Lettering Delights, Inspire Graphics
Scissors: Clouds edge, Fiskars

"New York City"
by Laura Kindron
Upland, California

SUPPLIES
Die cuts: Ellison
Pens: Zig Writer and Zig Millennium, EK Success
Lettering: Idea from *Creating Keepsakes'* May/June 1997 issue

Quick! Come look what we found!

March 1996

See, there's a little crab in here!

"Rocky Point"

by Sharon Lewis
Memory Lane
Mesa, Arizona

SUPPLIES

Stickers: Mrs. Grossman's
Craft punches: Marvy Uchida
Letter die cuts: Accu-Cut Systems
Die cuts: Crafty Cutter
Paper: The Paper Patch; Paper Pizazz,
Hot Off The Press
Scissors: Peaks, Mini-Pinking and Aztec edges, Fiskars
Pens: Zig Millennium and Zig Posterman (metallic), EK
Success

As we approached the bridge Katie went wild-this Katie all about... She looked up at it + said "It goes all the way up-to sky?!!"

Having a great seafood lunch!

"On the wharf"-Sandy, Katie, Mom, Diana, James, Billy + Bill

After Muir Woods, we went to San Fran. to meet Cindy, Suzey + family, Robbie + Dave, but they were too pooped to make it. It was packed here- too crowded for a cable ride even.

Alcatraz Island

Sourdough Bread!

We love the Irish Coffee at the Buena Vista. Billy treated us for Sandy's bday.

I love this town- it has so much character, great sites, great food, etc., but a summer weekend is not the time to really enjoy it.

San Fran. Skyline

"San Francisco"

by Colleen Erdmann Orkin
Van Nuys, California

SUPPLIES

Corner punch: Carl

Stickers: Mrs. Grossman's

Die cut: Ellison

Pen: Zig Millennium, EK Success

Bridge and mountains: Colleen's own design

INDEX